BETTER AS LOVERS

BOOK THREE IN THE CASSIDY AND CAHIR SERIES

JIMI GAILLARD-JEFFERSON

To our futures. May they be bright and full of friends

GET TO KNOW GUY

Spend more time with the most beloved character in the New Money Girls universe- Guy. It was love at first sight when he saw O'Shea. She...felt a little different.

This is a FREE novel. The link is in the back of the book. Happy reading!

CONTENTS

PROLOGUE

Cassidy (Before Cahir)

"What did it smell like?" He laid over me, weight heavy and familiar and pressing into me in a way that made it hard to breathe and perfectly okay.

I smiled at him. "What do you think?"

"I don't think with you. You don't know that by now?"

I traced circles and smeared the sweat on his back. There was something about Kevin that made me forget about the things-hygiene. Who was I to have a man's sweat heavy on my fingertips? To wipe it into my own body? To call it a keepsake and avoid the shower? Roll around in the bed and spread him. Call it sharing him.

Kevin always smelled like whatever I'd done to him. That was new to me. To have a man smell like the way I'd swallowed him. That smell was always softer. Deeper. Nails down his back smelled like dried red chili flakes. Riding him smelled like honeysuckle and newly lit charcoal.

Charred lemon when he wrapped his tongue around my clit.

It smelled like deviled eggs when I saw him with his wife. Mayonnaise and paprika and pickles and dill. The pickles were all wrong. Too much. They made the entire thing smell wrong. Too strong. An immediate reason to step away. But I didn't. Idiot that I was. I stayed and I watched. I watched him kiss her and hold her hand. I watched the smile bloom over her face. He hadn't said anything besides hello. But that was all she needed. To see him there, to know he was still hers and she was still his only.

I thought about going over there and breaking that up. I was in his clothes. I could have sat at the table and let that be enough. She would see and she would smell. Maybe she would smell what we'd done. Charred lemons that day.

It was all in my mind. I knew that. The smells weren't real. They were another trick I played on myself to make it seem like we were more than we were. To help me forget that there was always something not quite right with every moment we spent together. To make those moments better.

Even when he was gone the smells remained. They chased me in my dreams. They chased me away from sleep. I would press my nose into my sheets. Those smelled like me. And that made it hurt a little more. Gone.

I dreamed of his children. I smelled the toilet that night. The rancid, stark, acidity of vomit.

Because forever had a smell too. A combination of the two of us. Basil and rosemary and cashmere and raw silk. Decadence and newly turned earth and moments after a quick spring rain. It was a new smell and became my favorite even as I tried to deny it.

I felt it come up my throat with the bile. The shame. The ridicule.

Of course I denied the smell. Hadn't I known deep

down? Hadn't I known for months that he wasn't mine and never would be? Hadn't I known subconsciously he was married? Hadn't I known I was breaking the rules? I did it anyways. Put my hand in his and ran through the night and thought that I would get what I wanted.

So the universe took it away. So it showed me what I wasn't worthy of having. Because I broke the rules. Because I helped another break a vow. And maybe the universe would get him too. Maybe he would get his karma.

I didn't worry too much about that. I was too afraid, too consumed with figuring out how else I would be punished.

CHAPTER ONE

Cahir

Her hand shook before she put it in mine. She wasn't touching me, but I felt it. Probably because I shook at the exact same time.

I should have shut the fuck up. I should have put my hand to the small of her back and propelled her down the hall, to the elevator, to the car. I should have sat beside her while she put on her seatbelt. She might have picked music. She might not. She might have smiled back when I smiled at her.

But I didn't. Because I saw how much deeper, how stark, her freckles were when the color drained from her face. How she stood lost in her own closet, pants half on, when she realized she didn't have on panties. Sneakers without socks. My sneakers. Belt on backwards. Hair pulled back too tight from her face. She wasn't supposed to pull her hair back.

I'd never seen her pull her hair back.

So I asked her. Question couched in a statement of fact:

you don't have to do this. Her shoulders dropped when she heard my words.

I could hear everything. I heard the air leave our lungs. I heard our heartbeats. Discordant. And then she put her hand in mine and I didn't hear anything.

"We should get to the hospital," she said.

Then I did put my hand on the small of her back. I did guide her through a place that she'd walked before. She didn't smile when I smiled at her. She was too busy chewing a hole into her lower lip. But she was with me. I repeated that in my head like a mantra.

Cash is here.

We're together.

We're going to do this.

We want to do this.

Family. We're already a family.

Cash is here. She's not leaving.

Her hand slid into mine. I smiled again. Realer. And I settled.

"I don't think I should be in the delivery room."

The music was too loud. That was why I heard what I did. And because I wasn't paying attention. Cash always said I didn't pay attention to what she said when I drove. I would work on that.

"What?" The smile was still on my face. It hurt-the way it stretched and pushed at the muscles in my cheeks.

"I don't think I should be in the delivery room."

"Why?" You couldn't hear my smile.

"I don't-It's been hard enough for her, don't you think?"

"Her?" I almost choked on it. "Zion? It's been hard enough for her? You're thinking about-"

Her hand was still shaking. She wrapped it around my forearm. Or tried to. The steering wheel squeaked. My knuckles were white. And I wanted, for the first time, to be anywhere Cash wasn't. That want shot up my spine and made me wince.

"-it's been thrown in her face enough. Right? And this is a private moment for the two-"

"-people that are going to be raising Olivia. Her parents. Her mother and father. What in the entire-"

"Not at me, you won't." She didn't sound like she was smiling either.

"Then be you! Be Cash- goddamn- money for five seconds!"

I looked at her from the corner of my eye. Hair. That was what I saw. Hair pulled back tight for the first time. And her reflection in the dark windows. I eased my foot off the gas.

"Not every moment is for me."

Sanctimonious bullshit. "Every single one of Olivia's moments are for you. What the fuck are you doing right now?"

"You'll be there. You'll bring her to me. The moment-"

"I shouldn't have to bring her anywhere. It should be-" I inhaled. "Fuck it. Have what you want, Cassidy. Sit in the waiting room. Like she isn't yours."

I locked my jaw. Fuck it. Fuck it. Olivia was coming. Her ultrasound photos were the reason I couldn't keep my wallet in my pocket when I sat down. The reason my back-seat wasn't a place for papers and ties and whatever other bullshit I thought was important enough to take with me when I left the office.

She didn't deserve it. A fight. Anger. Not the first time I met her. Not even if it wasn't directed towards her.

There was no hand at the small of Cassidy's back when I walked into the hospital.

∞

Cahir

I didn't think she'd do it. I thought...

She sat down next to her mother, reached for her hand. Shook her head when Ms. May shot her a look that said a thousand words in less than a second.

And I stood there. Lingering in the waiting room because I couldn't- Who was she?

Who was I if I walked into that labor and delivery room without her?

There was Zion's mother, Tseday. A woman with grace. Class. Backbone like my mother's.

"Ma." I held out a hand, and she came. A woman, the only woman, that was always exactly who I knew she would be and whatever else I needed her to be.

A deep breath and we were washing our hands up to the elbow. I wanted to be clean the first time I held my baby. And it gave me another moment. A little more room.

Into the room. Dark. Huh. Some kind of ambient light. Deep purples and blues bounced around the room and over Zion's skin. She was on her back in that thin hospital bed. Thin like the chaise in her closet where she hid-

It didn't matter. Olivia did.

I repeated her name in my head like a mantra and stepped up to Zion's left side. Her mother on her right. We each took her hand. And that felt some kind of way but it didn't matter either. Olivia. And Cash. I was doing it for them.

I ignored the way her hand felt in mine. I didn't think about the way she smelled. The way the room smelled. I didn't let my body react to her screams that quieted down into moans. I didn't think about the way my knees went numb before my feet did and how my left shoulder blade itched, but I couldn't scratch it.

I didn't think about the sweat that beaded on my forehead. I didn't think about where Cash would have stood if she came in with me.

Fuck it. I thought about Cash. About the way she pinched my skin or dug her thumb into my palm the last time I saw Zion. I imagined it was her fingers gripping my hand too tight and turning it a mottled pink. I heard Zion's screams and morphed them into Cash's laugh. I knew I was sick in a way that required someone help me, but it didn't matter.

"Cahir."

Purple mixed in with the pale pink that was my hand. How interesting.

"Cahir."

My fingers tingled at one point, but that was over. Silence. Like a burn. Like that moment after I punched the glass.

"Cahir!"

I looked down at Zion and heard the mirror fracture. Saw the determination on her face to make me understand. It was there that night. It was there with her again in the hospital room. I didn't want it.

"Don't," I said. "I don't need it. I don't want it."

"We're having a baby." I didn't know how she pushed the words out. Her body shook the bed.

"Zion!" Her mother whispered something fast and low in a language I didn't understand. But I understood. I felt like the skin was flayed from my body.

"We aren't." My words were quiet. Her grip on my hand wasn't.

And so it went for a while. Her words. My silence. Her mother's whispers. My mother left the room.

Until Olivia crowned. Until she was there. And then in my arms. I cut the umbilical chord, and she was back in my arms. Her little eyes screwed shut. Her legs and arms moved. A protest to her recent eviction, and I understood. I smiled down at her.

And I forgot almost all of it. Except-

"Let's go get Mommy."

CHAPTER TWO

Cassidy

It followed me, and it never failed. I would go outside in the clothes my parents bought for me. Excited. Ready. There was something about just being in the world that brought a smile to my face. The possibilities perhaps. Ice cream. Lunch. Just us. A long drive and a visit to Gran. Maybe Gran would let me help in her shop. My grin would split my face.

And then it would come. "My God! She looks just like you!"

I had to tilt my head back to show whatever nosy adult dared to interrupt my time in the sun my displeasure. Lips curled so tight I might have been sucking on a lemon. My parents would smile at the adult. And I would know that I couldn't say what I wanted. I would not be permitted to say that it was my face. That I was short but I should have things of my own. That my parents had their own faces. That they should mind their gosh darned business and let me finish talking whichever of my parents I was with into taking me to the library or shopping. Shopping was better. Even if it was just the grocery store.

I wanted to belong to myself. I never felt like I did as a kid. Every time I got comfortable in my body it changed just a little. Height. Size. Skin. Voice. A little ass. Not enough tits. Attitude. A space of just nothing at all that panicked me. I filled it with nonsense things.

I thought the away camp my parents sent me to before I started high school would help. I would find myself. Or some version of myself that would get me through high school in Baltimore. I thought I would make memories if I couldn't make friends.

I didn't expect to make friends.

I didn't expect the pines to go on forever. I didn't expect to be in a bed so thin in a room with so many other girls. I didn't expect the empty space to come back. I didn't recognize it right away as longing. Missing. After I named the space, it took another day or two for me to identify what I missed. My parents. My familiar.

I didn't call them though when it was my time to step up to the payphone that didn't accept coins. No. I shoved my oversized iPod into my cut off jean shorts and called Gran.

She was better with my questions. Took her time with them. She was silent when I spoke except for the occasional "uh-huh" or "keep going, baby" when my voice tripped over a word or my eyes fell to the lyrics I wrote in permanent marker over my shell-toe Adidas and high-top Reeboks. She hummed while she considered what I said. Hummed the songs that didn't have words but that I knew intimately and always felt knew me back. Knew my soul.

"Can you see yourself? You got a way to do that while you're still on the phone with me?"

"I'm 14, Gran."

She laughed when other grandmothers, other grown-ups, would have gasped at my sass. I dug my iPod out my pocket while I let that laugh wash over me and fill up a little of the empty place.

"Look at yourself, my baby. You looking?"

"Yes."

"That nose you have? My husband gave you that. You make him real to me again every time you sneeze or draw your nose up when you smell. Those lips? Those are your mother's lips. But when you spread them in a smile you're her mother. Through and through, I swear. Your hair, all that hair, it's mine. Why I never let your mama mess with it, put perms in it. I saw myself as a little girl every time I parted your hair. I wondered if my mother was okay in her next life when I greased your scalp. I smelled her and smiled. I remembered the parties I went to. How I styled it for the days that mattered to me."

I ran my hand over my hair.

"You see those eyes? Your father's. You use them the way he does. To say things, funny things. To make decisions. To figure a person out. Your laugh is your mother's father's. He used to laugh til the joke wasn't funny and then just stop. Scared the shit out of me the first time I heard it. During a spades game. Do you understand, Cassidy?"

"I think so." I didn't. But I didn't want her to stop.

"There's no need to miss us. You are us and wholly yourself. You carry us with you no matter where you go. We're there. All the way down to your bones and working our way out."

"That sounds a little creepy, Gran."

She laughed. She always knew when I was joking. And she always laughed even when it wasn't funny. "Maybe it is. The way we pass things on like hand-me-downs. But you feel better, don't you?"

I looked at the face that was wholly mine and all of theirs. "Yeah."

"Good." I heard her smile and steeled myself. "Make sure you washing yourself good up there. You know them people ain't clean."

I'd heard and smelled a girl pee in the shower earlier that day and couldn't stop the snort and then the full laughter that came out of me. And Gran was right. I laughed until it was done then went quiet. I never knew either of my grandfathers but it was good to have pieces of them.

"I love you, Gran."

"I'll always love you, baby."

From then on I was different. What did I have to be afraid of if I carried so many with me? The best parts of them too. I took the pieces I wanted and twisted them into a whole new kind of thing. If that wasn't power, what was?

∞

Cassidy

Cahir's footsteps were soft when they came down the hallways but I heard them. And I stood. I let my feet move forward. For once I wasn't drawn to him. It was the bundle in his arms that moved just a little. Just a little. The fussing. Low and yet somehow the loudest thing I'd ever heard. It pushed out everything.

I didn't look down. I looked at him. I held out my arms. I felt the shifting of weight. The shifting of myself. For the first time since college, maybe, my body changed. My mind changed. I looked down at her.

And, oh, oh, oh. I felt the tears. I felt the wobble of my lips and the way I pulled air. I felt the way my heart kicked into overdrive. I felt everything. The tilt and spin of the earth. The gravity that bound me. The blood that flowed through me. And I gave it all to her. The first of a lifetime of willing sacrifices.

Olivia.

She was beautiful. She was perfect. I thought looking at Cahir, looking and loving, was the closest I'd get to perfect, but she was better.

Maybe because she looked like him? Not even an hour in the world and I saw her father. In her eyes. In the way her cries weren't loud but couldn't be ignored. The set of her shoulders. In the way she knew that swaddling blanket couldn't hold her. If she pressed a little harder, a little stronger, she could be free to grasp what she wanted.

I loved her. I would live for her. Die for her. Be the perfect mother to her. Give her whatever she needed and most of the things she wanted. And no one would ever tell her that she carried me the way Gran once told me.

CHAPTER THREE

Cassidy

I woke up with her. Not because Cahir's body didn't stir when Olivia murmured in her crib. No. His body seemed to be as attuned to hers as mine was. Slaves to her in just a few days. A few hours, honestly.

He didn't get up in the mornings, I thought, for the same reason that I didn't move in the night. It didn't belong to me. It was for them. The way dawn was for us.

I- oh, I got up. The moment I heard her. We fell into the routine that belonged just to us. She would whimper. The beginning of a cry. Her warning that it would get worse if I didn't appear. So I went.

My feet hit the ground first and bounced at the cold. I didn't remember the floors being so cold before. My palms went to my chest and my left thigh and rubbed in circles at the aches that were unfamiliar to me until Olivia came with all her perfection and said I was hers. I rubbed until the aches were dull. Embers instead of a full fire. I muttered the lyrics to songs that I used to listen to before- when Cahir and I went to the gym together. Motivators.

Then out the bed. Only a few dozen steps to the crib. We put it in the corner of his apartment, so the rising sun wouldn't be a shock to her face. She would never feel it burn her skin and know that she couldn't escape. It would be something that tickled at her, that gradually changed the space around her. She deserved to wake up that way.

My arms wrapped around my body while I took those steps. I wouldn't realize until I stood over her. Because of the cold, I told myself. I reached for her. My hands shook. That was the cold too.

Scoop. Retract. And then she was against my chest. I know the steps then. I don't even check her diaper. I know it needs to be changed. I hum the same songs Gran hummed for me. Even to my ears they sound off. But the whimpering quiets. That was enough. That was the bargain I made on the third morning: just let her be quieter.

In the videos I watched online, in the movies, mothers would smile at their babies. Make silly faces. Bring their nose in close and smell their baby smells. Tickle them. I hummed. That was all the bargain required.

I brought her to my chest and felt her lips move and her body seek. I couldn't tell her no, no, I don't have what you're looking for. I can't give you what you need. To the kitchen. Bottle of milk. Cahir and I didn't think about it before she was born. We didn't think of it at all until Tseday brought over bags of breast milk. I went back online. Of course, we'd give Olivia breast milk. Her moth-...

Breast milk. So much nutritional value. So good for development. For Olivia's immune system. The humming continued. Gran always hummed. I could too. For the entire time Olivia was awake, for the entire time she was in my arms, I could hum and never repeat a single song. Not for a day. Maybe not for a week.

The sites, the books, the doctors, the doula that came to us after, they all said the voice was important, that talking to her was just as important. It helped her brain develop. It helped her identify us, connect her to us. My throat was so dry in the morning though. Even though I was always swallowing.

I didn't have to think about how to make her bottles. I practiced so much before. And we had a routine. We knew our parts well. So there. The bottle was ready. Tested against my wrist. I always wanted something hotter for myself. Something to peel the skin away and show me pink. To fill with fluid for me to poke at. But that wouldn't do. That wasn't part of what I agreed to do if she would just be quiet. If she would just act like she liked me for a moment.

I shifted from foot to foot when she latched onto the bottle. Because it was good for her to have the movement. Because I couldn't find a comfortable place on the floors I danced all over with Cahir.

Hum.

Hum and hold back the tears. Tears were disruptive to the baby. Tears were disruptive to Cahir. Tears were proof to me.

I meditated with my eyes on Olivia. One big, audible breath. Three silent ones. Feel it all empty out, I said to myself. Then I pretended I felt it. Three deep silent breaths. Again because the first three weren't real. Shallower than a baptismal pool.

The next three counted.

I heard the ocean. Heard the rushing of water. A violent white noise. I heard every creak and moan in the apartment. I heard the elevator ding and cars twelve stories below us. I jumped like each of those noises were a surprise and not an every day part of my life. Jump and then freeze. Was Olivia different? Did I hear Cahir?

He couldn't know. He couldn't know when the bottle was done, and she was burped, that the whimpering would start again. Because he watched the same documentaries and read the same books I did. He knew that in the beginning that the babies emotions would be interlocked with ours. A mirror for how we felt. A beacon even.

Olivia knew. She knew I wasn't quite right. That I had the routine but nothing below the surface. The humming wasn't right and she deserved more. She deserved someone that was wholly there and not about to hyperventilate on their own air. Someone that could get it right and make it look easy the way her father did. She knew I was an idiot.

∞

Cahir

There was a moment after Olivia was born. A half an hour. Maybe forty-five minutes. I didn't want to bring Olivia home. Not if Cassidy was coming with me. She was there when I brought Olivia into the waiting room. I saw her face when she held her. I heard her. I felt her. The change. But still. Olivia was a miracle. A surprise. The best thing that ever happened to me.

I wouldn't bring her into a home where she wasn't wanted. She wouldn't be loved. But Cassidy was there to fasten Olivia into her stroller. She watched over me, her weight moved from the tip of one toe to another as I strapped the seat into the car. Before I could ask about who should drive she was in the backseat beside her.

Ok. Ok.

And then she was there in the morning. Before I could

get out of bed. I saw her hands shake, but didn't mine? And I heard the humming. I knew it. Like I knew her. I smiled and went back to sleep.

All I did was smile. I felt it grow throughout the day and into the night; my lips went numb. The nights were ours. Every three hours. A little cry. Strong. I was blessed to be surrounded by strong women. I felt a moment of delirium but that left easy. It felt like all the over-nighters I did developing projects. Pressing for deadlines. Energizing. Nothing like when I wondered if Cash would be mine again.

My feet were fast on the floor. I never felt them move. I didn't feel anything at all until I was beside her crib. She couldn't see me. Not yet. So I touched her first. A finger on her stomach. Another for her to grab and shock me again, as if it were the first time, with her strength. I would reach for her when she quieted, when she knew she wasn't alone. I'd use those moments to try and fix my face. My daughter had to think I was an idiot. My jaw was always slack when I held her. But I just-I knew she was real every time I held her.

I rocked her. Asked her if she were alright. Did she dream? Was she hungry? Did she just want to talk? What about? Books? Movies? Stocks? I was sure she understood them all already. No one who walked the earth was smarter than my little girl. She only gurgled a little and wiggled to remind me that it was rude to offer small talk when what she wanted most was to eat.

A bottle. Cash was better at them than me. Her movements soft and sure as she made them while she hummed. Her body always moving. Olivia would make little sounds back. Sometimes it was almost like she matched the humming. Olivia thought I didn't know, but she sounded different with each of us. Abrasive with me. Because I laughed over her. At her. I couldn't help it. I laughed at everything. Cried too. At commercials and billboards and stories in the paper and the books I read to Olivia at night. Charlotte's Web. Who knew?

She was gentle with Cash. Barely woke me in the morning. She curled in to Cash. Reached up and laid a little baby fist against Cash's neck. Kicked and fussed when I took her from Cash's arms. Probably why Cash looked so stressed when she saw me reach for the baby. I always riled her up.

Probably why I was so jealous of my nights. I knew Cash wouldn't take them from me. I wouldn't take her mornings. But still...

We danced after the bottle. Smooth movements. I wanted her to smile at me first but something told me- a mama's girl. Wasn't that a bitch?

When the dancing was over we sat down to a book. A movie. Olivia didn't like the movies very much at first. Hated Disney. I didn't blame her. The things they tried to teach women. I threw those movies out. And I realized I had to dim the TV. Then it was better. We could talk. In quiet voices- she was always a little quieter. Probably looking out for her mother. I still wasn't jealous.

Not at all.

I got a little ashamed of the time I spent angry on the way to the hospital, the hour or so before we brought Olivia home. I tried calling her Liv or Livie and they were both wrong. My baby needed her whole name. Or maybe Cash would figure something out. She was so good with her. Like she was born for it. I didn't even feel that way all the time. I was terrified the first few weeks. Cracked my knuckles so loud they sounded like gunshots whenever I approached Olivia. It was Cash that handed me diapers and laid her head against my back while I changed Olivia. I would feel her fingers move, mirroring my motions. I didn't question it.

I got phantom limbs every time Cash pulled Olivia out of her crib or off her blanket.

I wanted my baby too.

I saw her rubbing her chest and thighs. Felt more shame. Real shame. Of course her muscles were tired. She always had Olivia in her arms. Walked her from one side of her apartment or mine to the other. Up and down the stairs. Knew to strap her into her carseat and drive her around the block on the few nights she wouldn't settle. To give her a special music that came out of her bones. Even if it was a bit off-key.

I sent Cash to the spa. Bought every product they used when she came home empty handed. I washed her hair. I sent her shopping and knew what to expect. The next day everything she touched made it into her closet.

I bought her the Range Rover she deserved. She said it was too much. So I hired a driver. A better laptop and tablet for her business. Birkins. Too much. Cahir, she said and shook her head, it's all too much.

How? I smiled. Smiling was all I did. For the perfect mother? Was anything too much?

She always cried when I said that.

CHAPTER FOUR

Cassidy

Gran had to pry Olivia out of my hands. "Stop humming and give me my grandbaby."

"Great." I imagined roots growing out of my feet. Deep roots that would take hours to pull from the ground. Roots that trapped me and sent branches up my throat, to crowd my tongue. To block the truth.

If you take her everything will be undone. The bargain. She'll forget it.

I love her. I need her here. It hurts. I love her. Leave her where I can see her. You won't care for her like I will.

"Don't get sassy with me. Where's her bag?"

Cahir handed it to her. He packed the bag. I unpacked it. Checked it. Made sure everything was there. Re-packed it. Unpacked it again. To be sure.

Gran kissed my cheek. So did her hair. It felt like mine. She said it was mine. The piece of her I carried with me everywhere. Olivia's hair would-

The door clicked shut after Gran kissed Cahir, and it

was just us. He smiled at me and swept me up into his arms. "Alone at last!"

It was the same smile. The one he gave me before the hospital and the promises and the aches in my chest and legs. Before my feet found cold floors.

I thawed. I remembered I had a smile too and that it cost me nothing to give it to him. No bargains or bartering. Just a lifting of lips that met his. Over and over. From his kitchen to his bathroom. Into the shower. Hands on each other's bodies. Still the same, and new, and exactly the same. Kisses in the closet as we chose clothes for each other. Kisses on my fingers as we waited for the elevator.

I warmed. He turned on music when we both got in the car. He got out of the car.

"What are you doing?"

He opened my door and took off my seatbelt. I was out of the car. The music, my laughter, the click of my heels, they all echoed in the parking garage as we danced in a new place and made it ours.

How had I forgotten how much I loved him? Where had I put all those feelings?

He led me back to the car, and I felt like Cinderella.

"Another magic night."

He kissed me. That was how I knew he heard me. "Another one."

We both laughed. No need to actually tell the joke.

He drove us to the speakeasy with the live band and the dance floor that felt like it was supposed to be in a movie instead of the City. An oversized booth and too much champagne and lobster that almost melted when I ate it and course after course after course that only came when one of us shoved the other off the dance floor because we had to breathe.

Breathe.

Privacy in the booth. His hands creeped up my leg. Mine dragged down his chest and under the table and slipped my panties into his pocket. My back was pressed against the seat then. For just a moment. Long enough for me to lose my breath.

Breathe.

He fed me. I heard his zipper when I dragged it down. Felt the absence of air when he sucked it all in. Swallowed it when he exhaled. I smiled.

"I want to buy you a house."

My bracelet was the reason I couldn't pull my hand free fast enough. My greed was the reason. Forgetfulness. "What?"

"Don't you get tired of it? Moving from one apartment to another?"

No one noticed me in the chaos of traveling from one place to another. I couldn't get comfortable. If I couldn't get comfortable, I couldn't fuck up the bargain.

"No." I swallowed.

Breathe.

"It's nice to change," I said.

He laughed at me and brushed my hair back from my face. He was still before-Cahir and I was floating, untethered, from my own body. "We can't do that forever. We can't toss the baby back and forth between two places."

No. Only a bad mother, an unnatural mother, one that was pretending and hoping, would think that. "We can do whatever we want."

"We want to buy a house."

"No. We want to be happy."

"And houses make us miserable?"

Before-Cassidy would have laughed. Kissed him. Seen how ridiculous she was being and acquiesced. I rubbed my chest.

"Change does. Right now."

His arm was comforting when it draped across my shoulders. My body knew to shiver when he kissed me. "What's one more thing? We can hire people. Make it simple."

He told me about the service he found. The crew that would pack each of our apartments and move them into the house. The project manager and designer that would unpack for us and blend things.

"They do it all in one day," he said. "I won't tell you how much it costs."

Breathe. Be grateful to have an excuse for why your eyes were so wide. Grab hold of his laugh. Pray it will bring you back into yourself and stop the ringing.

"You sit down with the realtor and tell them exactly what you like." He snapped his fingers and laughed again when I jumped like someone fired a gun. So much laughter. So good for him.

Breathe.

"We could ask Guy. He's easy for you to talk to. And O'Shea would love to feel like she's masterminded another part of our lives." He sounded like he loved her. Like she was family. So nice for him.

Supposed to be nice for the both of us. There I was in the gown I was gifted because I was the perfect mother. Listening to plans for the house for the perfect family. So amazing.

Breathe.

Houses were just structures. They were nothing more. Losing a home was just losing a roof. Wasn't the loss of your center. Couldn't be used as proof to everyone that you were found out because there you had no ruckus or disruption to hide behind. Home wasn't just quiet nights. Home wasn't the beacon getting a little bright. Home was what you made it.

I fell back into my own body. And I smiled. I kissed his next words out of his mouth and washed away all of my rancid flavors with champagne.

"If you can talk, you can dance." I pushed at his shoulders.

Harder than I should have, but he was in the mood to laugh. Blessed enough to be able to. He took me back to the dance floor. I kissed him every time he tried to talk. His hands found my body and didn't leave it. So wonderful. So sexy.

CHAPTER FIVE

Cassidy

Before we made it into the apartment, the elevator, out of the parking garage, through the streets of the city, out of the parking lot of the speakeasy, out of the speakeasy itself, he was there. A thousand hands. A thousand sounds. A million tongues and tastes and smells. A million deaths. Tiny ones that shocked and rocked me and left me wondering if someone saw us. Someone besides my ancestors had to see us. We had to be on the verge of going to prison. Didn't they hear me panting his name? Begging him to wait? Just a minute. A minute. A second. Please, Cahir just- Fuck. Don't stop.

I tried to rip the clothes from my body and he- Bless him. He found a hand to stop me. To yank my hands away. He managed to keep his lips on me, drag his fingers down my leg, and to say "My body. Don't touch it without permission."

What used to be my body- now his body- came so hard it dripped down thighs that were also his. An extra set.

He made me drive. And pushed four fingers inside me. One at a time Then his thumb. When I got to a red light and threw a leg, a shoe that cost more than my monthly rent, over the center console, his hand shook.

"These seats will never smell the same," I said when the light was green and he was still.

He laughed and moved that hand again.

Thank the ancestors for brakes. For empty roads. For insurance. For the way his laughter warmed the darkness and laid over my skin just above the sweat that was just above the goosebumps that sprouted all over me. They were just above the shivers that ran down my legs and cramped my thighs.

"Drive." His voice was hard. The one he used before he hurt me. I deserved hurt. "I have things to do to you that I can't do in the middle of the street."

"I love you," I said.

Whimpered.

He laughed. So full of laughter all night. "That won't save you."

"I don't want to be safe." A truth. But only in that moment.

"I'll remind you that you said that." His hand shook again. "Drive."

I did. When I parked the car in his spot, backed in the way he asked me to, the first time his car was ever backed into the space, his hand had disappeared past his wrist. He kissed me and pulled it free. I didn't beg. I didn't plead. I knew better.

"Good girl," he said before he stepped out of the car. I knew whatever he did next would be a reward for me.

He opened my door and put a hand in the middle of my chest when I moved to get out. I opened my mouth. He pulled out his dick. I sat back. And watched.

It splashed on my gown. I wiped it away. I put my fingers in my mouth. I moaned. That-that tasted right. Better than right. It tasted like waking up.

My seat belt was gone. My legs were out of the car. One over the steering wheel. Thank God for yoga. He dove into me. Then pulled back to lap at my clit. Then formed suction around me and, and, and, and...

My screams bounced off the concrete and sprinted away. All of my screams did. A hundred meter dash to any ears that may have been nearby.

My hands were planted on the wall in the elevator. I knew better than to move them. I spread my feet wider. Pushed my hips back further. Held my breath. Worth it. When he slid in me. All of it was worth it. We rode the elevator up and down and up and down and he made me leave puddles on the floor. Every part of it. On the walls. I couldn't find it in me to be sorry or disgusted or shocked.

I let him lead me out of the elevator.

Alone. The first thought I had when the door closed behind me. All alone. There would be no humming. I could scream. No one would be louder than me. He would make me forget there was anyone but me. I would be the priority. I would be all he had.

My dress cascaded to my feet. A whisper of sound. "Please."

∞

Cassidy

I woke at the same time that I always did. When the sun was just about to creep up to the bed. I didn't listen for her whimpers. It was our routine. I rubbed at my chest. No shirt. I always wore a shirt to bed. After that day Olivia's head turned and tried to latch onto my nipple. Another thing I changed for her.

I rubbed my thigh. The same spot. I stood. And my whole body asked me what in the hell I was thinking. Aches and pains and the stretching of muscles left well enough alone. Oh.

There was my dress by the door. My shoes by the kitchen island. What was left of my panties were just a few feet from the door. And Cahir's suit, spread over the bed. Because I sat on the bed and took his clothes off, threw them behind me, whimpered every time he laughed and told me I could put my hand between my legs the way I wanted. Oh.

My pussy hurt. I sat down on the bed. And smiled the satisfied smile of a woman that had been battered, bruised, and destroyed in all the best ways. I smiled the satisfied smile of a woman that didn't have a baby waiting for her.

Oh.

His arm snaked around my waist and pulled me back into the bed. I squealed, laughed, moaned when he spread my legs and breathed me in. He was gentle. His tongue wet. His groans of pleasure louder than mine. His hair was soft when my fingers speared through it and tugged. His responding pinch made my body jump. He laughed.

I came. And floated. Oh, it was good. I wished it could be like this forever. Forever and ever and ever. Just him. Just me. No humming. Just my screams.

We could take it all back. Pretend we hadn't gone to the hospital. Get rid of the paperwork. Very quietly pass her along. She would never remember what we'd done. She would be relieved to be with someone else. Olivia wouldn't whimper anymore when she had a real mother.

I came again. I felt how it soaked the sheets, how much it surprised him, how happy he was.

He was inside me. His mouth by my ear so I could hear him over my begging and pleading and moaning and screaming.

"I love you. You're perfect."

"I-"

No. No. Shush, shush, Cassidy. Shut your fucking mouth. Tell him you love him while you consider ways to make his daughter disappear.

I looked at him. He…glowed. And it had nothing to do with me. It was her. Olivia. He'd been glowing since the moment the call came in. Since we were in the car. Even when I told him I wouldn't be in the hospital room- The glow never dimmed.

Didn't he see how much darker I was?

No. No, why would he? He was happy and when did happiness ever stop to see whatever it was that never left me. He would never let me give her away. He would hold her, and he would look at me. Maybe he would hold my hand. Maybe we would sit together with tea or water or wine. He would ask me what was wrong? What did I want? He would give me anything I wanted.

I would take a deep breath and gather my courage. I would let it all come out in a rush. I wanted him. Just him. Not who he was now. Who he was before it all happened. Before the elevator. Could we turn back time? Could it be just us again? He would shake his head and look. Shake his head. His mouth would fall open. He would ask questions. He would look down at her in confusion. He loved her so much. How could I not?

I would try to explain that I loved her. Of course I did. I loved her so much. I would fling myself in front of traffic for her. I would make bargains and hum for her. But I didn't like what happened in my mind when I held her. I didn't like the things I remembered. That wasn't right. That wasn't right. Could it be just us again? I liked him. I loved him.

He would say no. The sunlight would make the brown of his eyes startling. He would shake his head and say that there would always be Olivia. He would ask me to leave. Or he would leave. He would gather all of his things while he kept her in his line of sight. While he kept me in his line of sight. Because he didn't know who I was anymore. I wouldn't be offended. I wouldn't be able to find a way to explain to him that I didn't recognize myself either and once again he had the burden of another lost, delusional woman. But it wasn't his fault. He couldn't punch mirrors. He couldn't blame himself.

My body came for him. Again. He told me he loved me. Over and over. I let him assume that was the reason for my tears.

He held me but that wasn't right. He made me breakfast, and I hated him for it.

I turned down the volume of the television when he sat in front of it instead of coming back to bed- back to me. Easier than to remind him that there was a time when he wouldn't have turned the television on when I was naked in his bed. He would have been in it with me. He would have asked me to tell him my secrets and what I dreamed of the night before.

From there-

"What are you talking about?" He didn't even raise his voice. He didn't retreat. He came closer. Sat on the edge of the bed.

There was a time he would have laughed or poked at me or raised his voice. He'd become so much more patient since she came. How much more would she change him? What was wrong with me?

There was a knock at the door and I moved away from him. Because I knew.

I heard him. Heard Gran. Then I heard the voice he used for her.

I hummed when I reached for my clothes.

CHAPTER SIX

Cahir

Before there was Zion, and broken mirrors, and my promise that I didn't have room in my life for a child, before there were women that didn't matter unless they filled the empty space, there was Summer. She had the same red hair as my mother and a filthy sense of humor. She could turn any conversation, even the most innocent, to sex and make you feel like you'd done something wrong.

We did shots with breakfast and before we went out. We went out every night. To bars. Summer didn't dance. Then I found out she couldn't dance. It was the first time she was ever angry with me.

She couldn't cook and eventually I was tired of feeding her. She shrugged it off. She knew all the best places. All the ones that delivered at least. She couldn't be bothered with restaurants or anyplace where she couldn't talk as loud as she wanted. Any place where she couldn't shift her weight around from one foot to the other to whatever music blasted so loud talking was unnecessary. Just more shots.

My mother told me to never bring her home again after she met her. Not that it mattered. There wasn't a future with Summer. I didn't know why I introduced her to my parents. Because we'd been together long enough? Because it was expected? What was supposed to happen next? I thought time would bring the feeling that she was the one, or fate, or destiny, or some shit. Never came. And I never asked my mother why she didn't want Summer around. Not until Summer and I started fighting.

I got so sick of it I walked out of my own apartment. Went to my parent's house. Told the truth when they asked me over dinner what the hell was wrong with me.

"She's changed," I said. "She just wants to fight all the time."

My mother snorted. "No shock there."

"No?"

"No."

I'd never heard my mother be so curt before. "No…"

"Do you really not know?" She looked at my father.

He shrugged. "May be that he doesn't. Is there a reason for him to?"

"He went to college, didn't he?"

My father laughed. And I got tired of them talking around me the way they did when I was a child.

"What?"

Dumb of me to ask. As soon as the words were out of my mouth I saw what I'd been ignoring for so long.

Funny thing about the truth-it hides until it can't. And when it's done hiding it makes damned sure you can't look away. Of course. The little trips to the bathroom when we went out. The dazed moments. The runny nose. The high energy and swings from angry to happy to angry. The insistence that I not leave her alone. That we invite someone over, fill whatever place we were in with music. The twitches and exaggerations in her movements.

Obvious. All of it. I had gone to college. I was in tech. It seemed like everyone in my industry spent half their time in front of their computers and the rest of the time shoving a new way to get high into their bodies. And I'd told Summer, over and over and over again, that I wasn't like that. I'd drink as much as she wanted. I'd drink her under the table if it made her giggle. But I couldn't put shit in my body. I couldn't be with her if she did. I was terrified of the way it changed people, took away the best parts of them. I was terrified of losing my purpose, my ambition, my parent's pride. The little adopted boy, scared that he'd be alone one day, sent away, needed my parent's to be proud of me.

It was my fault. I knew that. And examined it on my way home. It was all right there. In the way she hid in bathrooms for longer than she should. And how upset she got when I touched her purse or asked where she'd disappeared to when we were out. I just didn't want to see it. I wanted to be happy more than I wanted to see the truth.

I said I would fix that. I said I would be different.

Then Zion came.

Then Cash came.

I never learned.

CHAPTER SEVEN

Cassidy

Delia didn't re-hire me. Not really. I showed up at Beyond with Olivia and all of her things. My files. Delia and I had a brief conversation. She told me to come back to work. I told her I'd already scheduled appointments. She held Olivia. Cooed at her. The woman that hated babies.

There was something about Olivia.

They all held her. Delia, O'Shea over her large belly, Nadia. Junie, last of all. Junie scooped Olivia up in her arms and walked out of Delia's office.

"Drama queen." I rolled my eyes and went to the Lonely Third.

Junie was settled on the couch. Her braids were fire engine red. Her bubble gum was grape. Olivia looked more alive than I'd ever seen her. She made little baby noises for Junie who talked to her, laughed with her, I was sure, and not at her, and kept Olivia from grabbing her braids or earrings. She made a game of it. I didn't know Junie could move so fast, that she was so good with children. My vision didn't turn green. I wasn't such a cliché. It was red. The same red of Junie's braids.

"Why didn't you tell me it was so bad? I would've come." She didn't look at me.

No one looked at me when Olivia was in the room.

I didn't blame them. I was too relieved to have the help, to have time to bind the fear. To know that the love I felt was real. I could keep it. Maybe I could enjoy it if I found a way to get rid of the rest.

"I didn't know how," I said.

She nodded.

I'd forgotten that about Junie in the time I'd been away from her. Everything about her screamed *Tell me, tell me. I'll never judge. And anyways, I already know. Just say it.*

"I thought if you knew you'd leave me. Cahir will when he finds out."

"Doubt it. That man would drink your piss if you asked him to."

The laugh felt wrong. Not because it wasn't real, but because I couldn't remember the last time I laughed.

Help me, ancestors. "I want to be her mother. I'm not. I can't…there's something in the way. I think she knows. I think she understands that I'm not Z-"

"-you know I'm adopted, right?"

I'd forgotten.

"My father is white. My mother's Black. At least that's her race. She's a pretty brown. Like oak. I would talk about my parents when I was in school. You know, the way kids do." She smiled down at Olivia who gurgled back up at her. "Then they'd come to school for conferences or plays or whatever and everyone would ask who they were. They couldn't see. Or they did see. And they tried to make me see it too. It worked for a little while. I got to wishing my skin was lighter, that I wasn't so black, so dark, that I looked like theirs. That I could pretend I was theirs."

She looked up at me, standing right there in the middle of the Lonely Third because I couldn't let my body relax. I couldn't stop rubbing my chest.

"I told my mother one day. She sat me down and said it wasn't looks that made me hers. It was that she said so. She said it. I was her daughter, and I would never be anything else no matter what anyone said, or how they stared, or what ignorant questions they asked. Because she loved me more than she loved anything she'd ever done, felt, seen, heard, or touched. Because everything in her belonged to me until after the day we both died and the earth ceased to exist. Because she goddamned said so." Junie came to me and put Olivia in my arms. "I thought that over. When my father came in and told me the same thing in his own way. And I realized they were right. Not because of how they felt, but because of how I felt. They didn't have to share my DNA. They just had to love me. I just had to love them. And I did. I loved them. And I wanted them to be my parents. So they were."

I nodded and looked down at Olivia. Her eyes were the same warm brown as her father. How comforting and delightful for him.

"If it were just about love, if it were just about whether I loved her enough I think-"

"Get your shit together, Cass."

I nodded. If it were just about how I felt about her it would be different. But there was something under the surface, I knew. Something that covered the love. Covered me and made me different and was so big and ravenous. Starving, I knew, for my attention. I couldn't give it that. I would lose everything if I learned what it was, if I learned to call it by its name.

∞

Cassidy

Home was an odd thing. I avoided mine. Because it was mine. My own place. My heartbeat. What would I do if I was around it too long? Who would I be? The woman that hummed? Or the woman that took the rose quartz of her keys and told herself she didn't have to go back even if he was hers and the baby was her love?

I said home was Cahir. Wherever he was with the glasses that he only wore after he'd admitted to himself that he worked too hard but would work more still. Because of Olivia. Because of me. Because he wanted us to have the best.

Home was the dinners I made so he wouldn't have to walk away from the work. Home was the smile on his face when he realized there was food and there was Olivia, with the noises she only made for him. The smiles. She gave all her smiles to him. Sometimes she still reached for me.

Home was that wide open space that wasn't quite right. Olivia's crib wasn't supposed to be in the corner. A temporary solution when we did it. Until, we whispered when it was just us and kisses interrupted every word. Until...

The energy was wrong. I felt it every time I walked in the door. A buzz of discontent. An itch to change and fix and rearrange. One Saturday I did. Cahir laughed. He always laughed. But he helped. It didn't matter though. The crib didn't fit.

It was nice to have something in common with the furniture in that apartment.

Junie said she wanted Olivia for a night. "Not in my apartment because, girl, could you imagine? But I'll stay at your place and watch her. Y'all go outside and experience it. You remember outside, right?"

We saw a movie. Horror. For me. He smiled every time I laughed. He laughed every time someone shushed me. Until it was a man that told me to shut up, called me a bitch. I had to put my hand on Cahir's arm. To remind him that we couldn't go to jail. It wasn't just us. He nodded.

"Keep your hand there. I need the reminder," he said.

I pulled down his zipper and put my hand in his pants instead. Felt his body draw up tight and felt powerful for a little while.

He threw away the bucket of popcorn we ignored and the sodas neither of us wanted to drink and took me to a gin bar. We sat under string lights on the back terrace. I had a botanical gin gimlet. I didn't know the name of his drink. I eyed it until he gave it to me and ordered another for himself with fake exasperation on his face. It was me that couldn't stop laughing that night.

"You're beautiful," he said over and over and leaned across the table to kiss me.

We ate and laughed and talked about the things that made us happy before we knew each other.

"Fighting," I told him.

He pulled back in surprise. "What?"

"I didn't dress the way I was supposed to. I didn't speak the way I was expected to. I didn't scream during horror movies and everyone knew my grandmother lived in the City and was basically a witch. They knew she taught me."

"Uh-huh."

"They thought it meant that they could treat me a certain way." I tilted my head. "I lost a lot at first. My mother wanted to put me in a different school. My father taught me to box. He said moving around wouldn't stop me from being different or people from being people. My mother's from Baltimore. My father moved there for her. So she knew better than to argue."

Cahir smiled the Olivia smile. It twisted me. Or the thing inside me twisted me. But not as much as it usually did. Maybe gin was the cure.

"I learned to fight. My father took me out to dinner when I got suspended for fighting. Because the loser never got suspended and I didn't have a cut on me. We went to the Prime Rib. He let me wear one of his blazers. My mother loaned me her Gucci belt then said I could keep it. She lied and said it looked better on me."

He kissed me. I was happy not to see the smile. I kissed him back. On and on and more and more until the separation between us threatened to kill me and I moved around the table and sat on his lap.

"We can't get arrested," I told him.

He laughed into my mouth and I got to have my drink in a new way before he kissed me again.

I looked at the moon when the kiss ended and thought maybe I could do it. Maybe I could be better.

"We're gonna have memories like that with Olivia," he said. "That's-you have no idea how much I want that. How much I'm ready for that."

I went back to my seat. His hand was there on the table, waiting. I was weak. I couldn't leave it empty even though I had an idea of what was coming.

"We're ready for a house, right?" His fingers squeezed mine. Did I pull away? Was that why he held on to me so tightly? "A place where there's room for each of us? That's intentional? Where you don't have to rearrange the furniture every weekend because the energy isn't right?"

Oh, he knew all my favorite buzzwords.

How to tell him that it was different in his apartment. That the chaos was a blanket that soothed. That wide open room that didn't feel quite right gave me so much room to hide.

That was the thing about houses. They were homes for families. More rooms and less places to hide. We had the largest house on the block when I was growing up in Baltimore and yet we were always running into each other, finding each other- conversation, touch, questions, seeing.

What are you doing? Let me see your homework. What are you working on, babe? Dad, what's that? Can I go with you? Mom, can you talk to Dad? He's being weird. The three of us making dinner or watching movies or listening to their old vinyls hum under the needle of the record player. It was my mother laid across my bed while I put outfits together. Us laid on the living room floor as we read Vogue together or sketched out outfits and then ran to her closet to see what she had to make them come alive.

He knew that. He had that growing up too. I felt it when I walked into his parents's home. Some houses are close no matter how many square feet they have. The love, the rightness shrunk them. Made you throw things out.

The thing about being seen was that once it happened you couldn't hide anymore. Like playing hide and seek with a child and knowing they will see you the moment they open their eyes. Because you can't make it hard for them. Even if you want to.

I would love home, and I would love Olivia, and I would love Cahir, and he would see what Olivia saw, and then home would be gone, and everything I loved would go with it. Because I didn't love myself. The gnawing thing inside me showed me that. I had lost a bit of love at some point. I had decided to be weak instead of growing that love again. Afraid.

Fear was familiar. I didn't know what the future was like but fear was an old friend.

I pulled my hand free of Cahir's. I heard my breathing. I heard my "no" and knew it was louder than the breathing. And I knew he knew.

CHAPTER EIGHT

Cahir

I woke her up earlier and earlier. Every morning. And I gave her a reason to have a body with sore thighs and a chest too tight and lungs that struggled to bring in air. I did it every morning until she reached for me before I was fully out of my sleep. Until it was her that made me beg.

"Let me take you to work," I said that morning.

She didn't smile. I was so busy laughing all the goddamned time I hadn't noticed that Cash didn't even smile. She didn't turn on the music that told me to stop work, to dance, to be present. She didn't laugh with Olivia or dance with her either. She just…hummed. I hated the sound of it. I wanted her to shut up. I wanted her to leave.

It terrified me. The leaving part. Because if she left I did too. It wasn't like when I was with Zion- when I knew I was drowning and convinced myself that it was the best thing for me, that I was going to die anyways and it was nice to have a choice.

Losing Cash would be…The future was what I made it. I always believed that. Until her. Then the future became whatever she agreed to. And that was safe in a way that didn't stifle or shrink me. That was okay. Because she loved me the right way. The kind of love that made her think about both of us before she said yes to me. I got to disappear, let go, fly. I didn't think about the weight that might have put on her. Because I thought she was as strong as she was soft. I thought it would be fine because she would tell me when it was too much. I would come back to earth for her. I'd walk with her. Maybe I'd be the tether that made it possible for her to fly. But no, not really. Cash didn't need that. She could fly on her own. She'd always known how.

I panicked first. I couldn't lose Cash because I wanted to fly. How was that better than what Zion did to me? Stay, Cash, my panic suggested, because that will make me happy no matter how you feel. Even if it crushes you stay so I can keep my smile.

Shame. I didn't want to be what cut me deepest. I didn't want to look down at Cash's hands and see scars. I didn't-

The truth was I didn't know how to pull my head out of my own ass to fix it. I knew sex. I knew her body. I knew her gasps and her moans and how her body relaxed in spite of her stress after I gave her more orgasms than she thought she could handle. So I gave them to her until I realized I didn't have a better plan.

I took her to work. I watched her walk into Beyond. I waited until she went up the stairs and Junie was back at her desk. I waited until Junie came to my window.

"Come on," she said. Candy-sweet cherry gum breath wafting over my face. "You been waiting long enough to say what you want to say."

I got out of the car and followed her into Beyond.

∞

Cahir

"I like your hair," I said. It was teal. A good color against her skin.

"You're supposed to." She sat at her chair and ignored the ringing phone. "Talk."

"Do you need to answer that?"

"No. It's a man. The men never make the decisions here."

"Oh."

"Talk."

"Right."

"This. This is why the men never make the decisions around here."

I laughed and perched on the corner of her desk. "I'm losing her."

"She's been lost since she found out Zion was pregnant. Come on now. You blind? Stupid? That naïve?"

"We fixed that."

"No. You talked about it a whole lot. After she broke up with you. Y'all back together?"

I couldn't blame it on Olivia. I couldn't point to the fact that I had a new born. It was my fault that I missed that one

"Crazy thing about the two of y'all is how much you don't wanna talk then you do wanna talk but you don't talk about the shit that's actually important. Y'all talk about your feelings."

"Feelings are important. They're how you build trust."

She snorted, and I felt like I'd just been cursed out. Thoroughly. "Feelings don't mean shit. Decisions do. Got all the feelings in the world but can't decide to fix this shit."

"I don't know how."

"Finally." She softened. "The truth."

"I don't think she hates the baby." Everything in me drew up tight.

"No. She loves Olivia."

And released.

"I don't think she likes her though."

Bile rose in my throat.

"It's not as bad as you think. A lot of new mothers don't like their kids. What is bad is that you was so ready to buy into the idea of this little United Colors of Benetton family image that you didn't even check in with her."

What was I supposed to say to that? I looked at my shoes. The ones Cash picked out for me and made sure were always perfectly shined.

"Only reason I haven't whooped your ass is because I know you ain't doing it on purpose."

"Tell me how to fix it. I can't lose her." The truth made my voice dull.

"What do you think it was like for your parents in the beginning?"

"Huh?"

"When they first adopted you. You were a baby, right?"

"I don't know."

"I think it takes either a certain kind of entitlement or courage to adopt a kid outside your race. To get a kid that don't look like you. Everyone knows. The kid knows. You can never pretend. Can't lie. Kid knows in some ways they aren't yours. You know."

"She's ours."

"She's yours. For sure. She looks like you. She'll never look like Cash."

I wasn't dumb enough to ask if that mattered. I was dumb enough to have never considered it.

"I think there has to be a lot of pressure. What if you get

it wrong? You don't have biology to lean back on. Can't say 'I gave birth to you so it doesn't matter if I don't get this right.' You chose the kid. Could've left them alone. But you chose. And now you've got to get it right. What if it doesn't click into place?"

I nodded. Because I didn't understand but was sure I would if she just kept talking.

"In your parents's case they could share in it, right? Like a tag team. Help when the other is floundering. Take some kind of comfort in knowing the person beside you has the same fears as you. Y'all are really in it together." Junie tossed her braids over her shoulder. "But y'all aren't in it. Cash signed some papers that say Olivia is hers. She's trying to feel it. From the beginning Olivia just was yours. Everyone knew it. Just asked to be polite."

I remembered O'Shea on my counter, behind my desk. Never going away. Voicemail after voicemail after text message. Because, yeah, she knew. I remembered the way my mother and my friends asked about Cash, scared to assume but doing it anyways. Assuming that she left. Surprised that she stayed and what she was willing to do. Questioning if it was the right choice. If we thought it through.

Yes, I told them. This was what we were going to be. It was just happening sooner than expected. A little out of order. The women would soften. Men would slap my shoulder, my back. Congratulations from everyone. For picking the right woman. For getting my happily ever after.

"So here she is trying to get right but shit, a newborn baby is hard for biological mothers. And she's not just holding some baby. She's holding the thing that broke up y'all's relationship. She's holding your relationship with Zion. From beginning to end. There she is holding the evidence of the woman that broke you, broke what you and her built, and in some ways broke her. What she supposed to do? Skip into the sunset? Say it's all easy and keep her cool?"

I should have stayed in my car.

∞

Cahir

It felt like a drug deal. We met in the back of a Target parking lot. The last row of spaces in the far corner. The concrete kept the sun and the wind and sometimes the rain away. We didn't talk. Tseday, Zion's mother, would hand me one of those oversized lunchboxes, icepack and all, full of breast milk. I would hand her the empty lunchbox she gave me the week before and a room temperature icepack. In the beginning I would feel guilty that it wasn't frozen, but what the fuck did I have to feel guilty about?

It was the worst part of my week. It was the only thing I wouldn't let Cash share in. It was the only time I was happy to leave Olivia at home.

It hit me in the chest every time Tseday got out of her car. She looked like Zion which was its own kind of ache. I could see Olivia in her. That hit me like a fist to the chest. Every time. A surprise every single time. Loss of air. Rounded shoulders. Watery eyes and ringing ears. Off balance and feeling stupid because anyone could see how I got sucker punched.

But it wasn't about me. I told myself that over and over and over again. It wasn't about me. Everything wasn't about me. Wasn't that why Cash and I were in such a fucking mess? Because I thought it was? And even with the evidence right there I still struggled. Still wanted to tell someone how unfair it all was and how much I hated it. Still wanted to stay in my car and pretend I didn't see her, didn't need her, could cut myself off from that entire fucking family and finally move on with my goddamned life.

I took a deep breath and opened the car door.

"Hello."

I lied. Sometimes Tseday spoke.

"Zion is better. Less of the tears. She asks after you. After the baby." She tilted her head. She stood in front of her open car door. The car was still running. Because it was supposed to be quick. A frugal woman despite her wealth. I knew she knew she was wasting gas. And my time. But why would my time matter? Why would I? "I am wrong. She cried when she knew the baby's name was still Olivia. She called out for you."

"Here." I gave her the empty bag. I held my hand out. I wasn't, in that moment, who my mother raised me to be, but she probably never thought I would be in that kind of situation.

"Cahir." She reached for me. She knew I couldn't do that. I stepped back. "I know I do not deserve to ask but- The sounds of my daughter."

"Yeah. I remember." I rubbed a finger over my scars. "Why? Why are you asking me for anything?"

A ballsy woman. She didn't bow her head. Didn't blink. Strength. It didn't matter. I had Cash to teach Olivia that.

"I-" Her hands smoothed over an already perfectly smooth skirt. "May I know the child?"

"You've got to be shitting me." I held out my hand again. "Give it to me."

"Cahir-"

"Tseday. No. Are you insane? No." My head spun a little. I had to go. I had to leave before I felt my knees give out and my body hit the pavement and everyone got to see that despite everything I said I wasn't okay and I didn't have shit together. "Give it to me or let me go buy formula."

She put the bag in my hand. I kept myself from tossing it across the driver's seat and not giving a shit where it landed. I kept myself from flinging myself in to the car and speeding away.

Barely.

"Think about it." Her voice wasn't loud but her words carried. A family gift.

I smelled burnt rubber when I pulled out of the parking lot.

CHAPTER NINE

Cassidy

In the dream, Olivia was there. The chubby cheeks and excitement of a child on her first day of kindergarten. Her hair was decorated with colorful barrettes and she hopped from foot to foot. She laughed. It sounded like mine. That was why I stopped humming and turned to see her. Because the laugh was so like mine I had to make sure it didn't come from me.

She reached a hand out to me. Fingers spread wide the way little kids do-so they feel all of us, grasp a little more, hold on a little tighter. I wanted to reach for her too. She looked so happy. Loved. She looked at me. Like I was responsible for it. Like I got it right.

I reached. Darkness swept over my fingers. Between them. Tendrils of it. It coated the floor. Slick, slow moving. Moving to my baby. It held me back. Held me down. It amplified my screams as I watched it drown her.

I woke up in silence. I breathed. I waited for Saturday to begin. For the routine to begin.

He left early. Rolled out of bed and showered, groomed, dressed. He was so quiet I thought I dreamed it in that half space between awake and sleeping. He was gentle when he kissed me goodbye. A kiss on my lips that reminded me, in an instant, that morning breath, crust on my face, satin cap askew, I was desirable. I was desired.

He fed the baby. Changed her. Gave her words and hushed laughter and an admonishment not to "wake Mommy up." Olivia was back in her crib, and he was gone.

Every other Saturday when he left to see Tseday and exchange lunch boxes like children on the playground that wanted to be friends but didn't dare to hope, I laid in the bed for as long as possible with my eyes screwed tight and my hand over my mouth. I didn't want even the air to move. Let her stay asleep for as long as possible.

Not that morning. I got out of the bed that morning. I picked her up. I held her. I filled her baby bath. I didn't hum. I thought about it. I almost did it. Mouth open, lungs full of air, head full of melody. Instead I sang the last song Cahir and I cooked to. Sang it over and over and over again until my feet wanted to move. I played it. She bounced in my arms. So I danced.

I had to refill the tub, but that was okay. The way my hand shook was okay too. Shakes happened when you went slow. And I was. Slow to rub the little cloth over baby soft skin. Slow with shampoo on hair that filled in quickly, darkened, lengthened. Slow to rinse. Slow when I sang. Slow when I smiled.

She was fast when she smiled back. My tears were fast when they tracked down my cheeks.

I dried her. Dressed her. She fell asleep, and I thanked the ancestors. Too much. Too much. Too much to hold.

I got into bed and drifted back to sleep. I was tired of tired. Tired of sleep.

Cahir came home. I heard his clothes when they fell to the floor. Jeans and a belt that wasn't freed from his pants. A t-shirt. I had to concentrate to hear that one. Socks. Boxers. I heard those. Oh, I heard those.

His arms were around me. His smile was pressed into my neck. I didn't have a smile to give back to him. I was so tired of tired. But I was glad he was there. Glad his arms were what I remembered. Glad he didn't ask if I was okay as if I could remember what okay was.

"Tseday asked if she could see Olivia. Have a relationship with her." There was no smile pressing into me.

His arms were tight. I couldn't turn. Couldn't see him. How could I give him the anger that bubbled up in me and wanted to ooze out of my mouth like sludge if I couldn't look him in the eye?

"I don't want to do it," he said. "I told her no. It wasn't a decision for me to make on my own though so…"

"I can't." I couldn't sound like I had my shit together when I said it either. "I can't give her you and the baby and-"

"I thought so." He kissed my shoulder. "I thought so."

I knew he said everything was okay. I willed my body to believe him. To stop my heart from racing and the blood draining from my feet so fast it left a tingling sensation that was offset only by the pounding in my ears and the tightness in my back and thighs.

"We won't do it." His kisses trailed over my ears, my neck, my shoulders. His fingers pushed the muscles of my thighs until they relaxed. Until the only ragged things about me were my breathing and my tears.

"I'm sorry." I choked on it. Forced it out. I couldn't watch Olivia drown. "I can't fix it. There's something wrong with me."

"No. There isn't. There's something wrong with us. Can we talk about it?"

CHAPTER TEN

Cahir

Her tears stopped. Just like that. And she was still. She was there. The Cash I fell in love with carried an energy with her. Playful, frenetic, barely contained anger, curiosity, impatience, love, loyalty, and a desire to compete with herself first because she didn't believe anyone else could really keep up, defiance. I didn't notice the absence of that energy until she went still. I didn't realize how much I missed her.

"I think I know what's happening, Cash. I think. But can you tell me?"

There were the tears again. The shaking.

"I love you. I'm going to tell you what I think. And then I'm going to tell you I'm not leaving."

She hiccuped.

I loved her. "I think it's not about the baby. I think it's us and I think it's us because of me. And I think you don't want to-Why do you think I'll leave you?"

I had to let her go when she curled into the fetal position. I had to fill my fists with our sheets and feel the help-lessness that comes with having a solution and knowing it isn't going to be right. Not if you offer it.

"I love her," she said when the tears stopped. Her body still shook. "I do. I want to be there. I had this...There was a moment in the hospital-She's never going to look like me."

I thought about touching her. Just a hand down her back. A kiss dropped on all that hair. But I remembered what it was to be touched when it felt like everything inside of me had finally broken. Fist. Sheets. Slippery because of the sweat. The effort.

"It's not important. I know I should know that. But it was just-every time I look at her it's like I remember that night. I'm in the elevator again. I just want to get past it. I want-But then I feel like I'll never get past it. Like everything I do with you is just some kind of karmic payback for being with Kevin. Cause I kind of knew he was married. Or at least that something wasn't right." She shuddered when she breathed. So still I almost worried. I almost reached for her. "I thought Kevin would be over. I ended it. I did the right thing eventually. I thought I was right because I got you. And then you did that. You lied to me too. Hid from me too. And I realized no, no. The cycle is going to continue."

I knew about that. The guilt that you didn't deserve what you had. It came to me every time my parents forgave me when I was a child. Came back when I got Cash. Receded when she left. It was almost...soothing. To know that I was finally going to pay for all my mistakes. To know that the inevitable had finally happened. I didn't have to worry. I didn't have to tread lightly anymore. The bottom had fallen out. I could do it. I could prove I deserved Cash. I could prove I deserved the future I made for myself.

Except...

"I can't-I can't make you tell me the truth. I can't make you treat me like a partner. I can't make you stay or stand in the open where I can see you-all of you. So I'm going to be a good mother. That's what I decided. I'm going to be a good mother. Except she looks like you and her, I think. And it stops me. I love her. Then one day I love her more. Then one day she's everything. Then you decide I'm not, and everything is gone. I didn't put myself together last time. I just came back. What would I do if you left again?"

"I'm not leaving."

She laughed. She laughed like bullets confident in where they were going and the havoc they were going to wreak. She laughed like she knew she could kill me and thought she should. For fun. For justice. For a bit of balance in an otherwise uneven and shitty life.

Ok.

"What? How in hell would I know that?"

The baby cried. Cash moved before I did. Leaned over the crib. Just put her face close enough to Olivia's and there was silence. Whispers between the two of them. I heard their smiles. And I-

Fuck.

I carried dualities once. I held Zion and loved her as much as I hated her. Wanted to get close as a way to figure out a way to get away. A way to figure out the hold she had on me so I could detangle it. A way to figure out the love I had for her so that I could get back to it, that pure place, even though I knew we would never be the same again. Stay and go. It wore me down. I stayed silent through it. Cash had to hum.

She got back in the bed. No more laying down. She faced me. I sat up to face her. She scooted closer. Our knees touched. She took off the satin cap. Shook her hair loose. Looked at me.

Okay.

"You don't. I do. I know what the consequences are because you taught me. I know what waking up without you day after day feels like. I know what sleeping alone is like. I know what not being able to talk to you feels like. Not being able to touch you." I leaned forward and found my favorite of her curls. I wrapped it around my finger. She smiled and leaned into my touch. "I know what it's like to know it's funny and know there's no one that would laugh with me the way you do. I know what it's like to have a thought that no one but you would understand and know that you won't show up. You showed me your boundaries."

I dropped my voice and hoped she remembered the night she made me watch her favorite movies. "You showed me the gun line, boss."

She laughed.

"Beyond that, we're a family now. I get why-" I shook my head. "I get that it's been tough and you aren't sure. But Olivia is yours. Not because of the paperwork or because I want her to be or because-You say you're struggling, but you should see yourself with her. She's yours. I can't take her from you. I wouldn't."

I didn't catch her tears. She didn't either.

"If I mess up you and me, I mess up you, me, and her. I can't say I love Olivia and not do and be everything I'm supposed to be for you."

She crawled into my lap, and finally, finally, I held her while she cried.

CHAPTER ELEVEN

Cassidy

I'd always known when it was time to go. Always.

A simple reach for my things. Panties back on. Where were my heels? There. I stood in them. At Beyond, I packed up my files. At Kevin's-well, there was never a time, he said, that was right for me to be in his space. But I left him. I walked away again and again even when he asked and justified and begged. Head high. I knew what I deserved. I knew what I wanted.

I should have left Cahir when he told me about Zion. Not the peeling out of the garage or the online profiles. Not the first date. None of that. I should have sat in the sadness. I should have done without him. Hurt until the numbness set in. Stayed numb until the day the feelings broke back through. I should have. I should have believed I was strong enough to sit in the dark until the sun came again. I should have believed that I could be his friend, just his friend. I should have remembered that trouble don't last always and everything has an expiration date. Seasons and reasons. Longing didn't matter. What was best for me was. Sometimes sadness was best.

Instead I decided to love him. Instead I decided to lay in his bed or mine and whisper in tones too quiet for him to hear that I would try one more time. But I was bruised. My heart was so bruised and I didn't want to fix it alone and I didn't have the words to show him where it hurt.

Anger wouldn't guide him. Fear wouldn't help him fix it. If I wasn't going to leave, if I was going to call his baby girl mine and let her own every part of my heart that didn't belong to him, and didn't have room for me, I would have to fix it.

I didn't want to. I wanted to be angry. I wanted to stew and fight. I wanted to hide in my misery and revel in pointed fingers. I wanted to feel the bitterness grow and list reason after reason for why it wasn't my fault. I wanted to fight through smiles and sleep. Darkness and quiet around me. I wanted to hum.

I wanted the half in, half out. I wanted a family and an exit strategy. I wanted the familiarity of fear.

That was why I cried in his lap. Anger was for the victim. Growth was for the survivor. Release was for the survivor.

∞

Cahir

Days of sitting, wondering if she heard me or if my words didn't mean anything at all. Days of watching her smile at the baby, whisper to her, dance with her. Slow dances. Not the blur of feet and arms and hips that I knew she held inside of her.

Who was she being gentle for? Who had she slowed down for?

I went back to work. My office was too big so I ordered a crib and toys and things. Things I thought Olivia would like and I brought her to work with me. I held her in my lap during business calls and team meetings. I took her with me and took all of the jokes, the questioning looks, with a smile.

I made us dinner. Every night. It was on the table when she came home. Or a dress. Sometimes there was a dress on the bed for her and a question in my eyes and a tightness in my shoulders and back until she nodded and said yes. She never smiled when she said yes.

I'd take her out. She didn't want to dance. Dinner, then. Shows. Comedy shows. Plays. I took her to see an illusionist and wished I could capture the looks on her face. The looks on my face when she reached for my hand.

It was different—doing it for the second time around. The first time I didn't understand until I was in it. I didn't know what I did wrong. I didn't know what she thought. I didn't know that it wasn't fixed. I didn't know how deep losing her went. I didn't know the baby wouldn't make it easier.

Having someone we loved in common didn't make us love each other any more. I could wrap an arm around her waist and stand with her, smile with her, at Olivia. Olivia's eyes would close and Cash would be gone.

But dinner. She was with me then. And breakfast. And lunch. I obsessed over food as much as I obsessed over her. Over the nights my hand traced over hers until her body was flush with mine and her air was all I had, and wanted, to breathe.

That day, she woke me with it. The first time in too long that her hands were there when I woke up. Possessive and sure that what was on me was built for her, just her. And her pleasure. No hair to tickle my ear. Just the softness of satin. Just her lips on my neck.

"Let's get a house."

I was awake and harder than I'd ever been in my life. So fast it made me dizzy. So fast she gasped and moaned and moved in ways I knew she didn't mean to when I slid inside her.

"Say it again." My voice pitched lower. To feel her body contract. To ensure I didn't wake the baby.

"Let's get a house."

"When?" A nudge. Not even a push. But I heard her. Smelled her. Felt her sigh and the way her eyes rolled back in her head.

She kissed me. Another nudge. She moaned into my mouth. Tartness of early morning and underneath that there was her. I got high on it. Wanted more of it.

I filled my hands with her. Back. Hips. Shoulders. Pushed. In and out and in again. Part of me hoped I'd find the part of her that didn't feel like heaven and made me comfortable with going through hell for her if it was what she wanted.

It was her nails in my back that brought me back. "When?"

"I- Cahir, please."

"No." I whispered and dropped kisses on her jaw. "No. You started it. Finish it. When?"

"When we find the right house."

I laughed. And went still. She wrapped her legs around my hips and let her knees open wide, wide. Because she knew. She knew what made me lose my mind. She didn't know, hadn't considered, how much crazier I felt when I thought that she might not come back. How it made me want to peel away and crawl out of my own skin.

"Do better, Cash."

"Now. Whenever you say. Please."

A thumb on her clit. A whisper of touch. It didn't need much more. She was so wet. Hot. She would leave marks on my back. If I didn't kiss her, she would wake Olivia.

"You're gonna live with me?"

"Yes. With conditions."

Even that sounded sexy. It dropped like a brick in my stomach, but it didn't make me stop. Her moans in my ear, the way I felt her spill over and around me, the burning in my back and thighs, the absence of time and space and light. I didn't stop.

When I asked her for answers, I wanted her to remember who the fuck I was.

Cassidy

Fuck. He could just...And I would just...leave. Float into another place where there was only me, but I wasn't me. I was larger than galaxies and more powerful than any god that I'd ever read about, and content to do nothing but float. Float as I came down from the high, from the flying.

His smell was what came through first. It never smelled any different with Cahir. Just him. My tether to reality and my self. He brought the warmth back into me and made me want to do more than float. He made me want to see. And when I saw him- on top of me, under me- I wanted to hear. His breath. His laugh at how absolutely insane every second of us together was. His whispered "I love you, Cash." I heard, and then I wanted to feel his heart beat against mine. His body to be both hard and soft and know that it was because of me. His hands as they found the places I didn't know would hurt in a minute or an hour or a day and massaged them into compliance.

How could I compare smelling desserts and fruit to that?

It would've been easier for me if Cahir weren't better in every way, if I didn't know it.

He pulled out and away. Soft feet crossed the floor to the bathroom. Gentle hands rubbed a warm cloth over my body. So much of me was his that I didn't blush anymore when he did it. Why shouldn't he polish his trophy?

He laid beside me and I rolled and rolled until my body sprawled across his and his arms wrapped around me and held me in the place that I wanted most of all. His chin rested on my head. I laughed, quick, subdued, when he took off my bonnet and fluffed my hair. I let myself forget. Forgetting the past was easy. In the early morning when it was just us I could forget there was a time before. The present...I was strong. I could always forget when I wanted to.

His hands traced patterns over my skin. "We didn't really prep for this."

"Hmm?"

"The baby. We got rid of all the sharp edges. Covered up the outlets. Read the books. Went to the classes. Annoyed the doctor. We did all of that."

"Mm-hmm."

"But we didn't really do anything to get us ready."

My eyes wanted to open. I shut them. I screwed them shut. No.

"Every married person I know says that babies don't make it better. They show you all the places you've gone wrong. They show you all of the things you don't like."

I had to breathe. He would know if I stopped.

"We didn't get ready. I'm sorry for that. I'm sorry I thought that we could just go skipping into this and be great at it. We could just forget all the other shit because it didn't matter. Because we were us, and we had this, and nothing else mattered."

I was so sick of fucking crying. Fucking exhausted. Annoyed that he always knew when to let me cry, hide my face, and just be close to him. Annoyed that in the little ways he never got me wrong.

"So now we're in this thing, right? And I want to take a couple steps forward. But we're not in the same place. We're together but- you know?"

I nodded and wiped my tears off his chest. A broad sweep of my arm. He laughed.

"I take a step forward. And maybe you do too. But my step and your step, even though they happen together, don't put us in the same place"

I nodded again and felt like an idiot for it. "Yes." The word sounded like it hurt. It did. But being seen, hearing the truth even if you're ready for it, those things always hurt.

"So the house. Tell me what you want."

"I-" I wanted him. That was the truth. I loved him. That was even truer. I wanted a family with him. I wanted the fairy tale ending. I wanted to get my fucking shit together. I wanted the tears to stop. The crawling sensation that everything was wrong. The heat behind my eyes. The heaviness in my tongue when there were so many words that felt like the right ones to explain what was happening to me. The hurt in my thigh and chest.

"Take a minute if you need it."

Stupid to be mad. But I was when he said that. And I used the anger to push a bit of the truth out. "I need to be alone sometimes. Sometimes the two of you are too much and I need to run before I go insane wondering if you will."

"What's that mean?"

"My own bedroom which is weird if we're back in a

relationship." I stopped. Better to ask. Better to know and be done with it. Fuck it. "Are we back in a relationship?"

That was when he touched me. One hand ran over my hair. The other down my back. "I think you're the one that needs to answer that question."

CHAPTER TWELVE

Cassidy

I t took me five days to realize how mad his non-answer of an answer made me. I was the only one that could answer that? Weren't we in this shit to-fucking-gether? Why did everything have to get tossed onto my shoulders? Why did I have to swoop in and-

"Can you grab the plates?"

He cooked dinner every night. Like that made it better. Like he could just do that one little thing to remind me what we were before he decided I was in charge and he didn't have to do a goddamned thing but show up and give me words I couldn't do boo-shit with.

Grab the plates. Like they weren't six fucking feet away from him. Oh. An excuse to touch me. To wrap his arms around my waist and-Nuzzle my neck? Could've put his face in my pussy if he was going to make me get up from the couch and leave my wine behind.

Selfish. That's what a person had to be to just...

"Silverware, Cash."

Oh, now I was a busboy. Now I was working in a restaurant. Weird. No one showed me a menu when I walked the fuck in.

Silverware on the table. Water glasses too. And fuck it, let's use the nice napkins. Let's light a few candles. Let's get a wine glass for him and just put it-

I didn't make a noise when the glass broke and sliced through my palm. Not a gasp or a hiss or a shriek. But he came over anyways.

"Go away," I said.

"Let me see it." He angled my hand towards the light.

Uh-huh. So fucking willing to fix this but when it's time to fix the other things I get told that it's all on me.

"Don't move." He rummaged around in the bathroom and came back to me.

"No. Of course not. I'll just drip onto the table. It's fine. I love it here."

"The table is glass, Cash. Easier to clean than the floor or-" He pushed a pair of tweezers into my cut.

"What the fuck is wrong with you?!"

"Stop it. We already have a baby. We don't need you to be one too." He held up the piece of glass he fished out of my cut.

And made me aware, really aware, of all the blood. "No. No. I'm supposed to be the one finding all the fucking answers."

He didn't do anything but shove those tweezers back into my fucking hand like I didn't have any nerve endings and couldn't feel any pain. But he'd always thought I was invincible, hadn't he?

He pulled out another piece of glass. "One more. Try to hold it together for a few more seconds."

This motherfucker. "I've been holding it together since I met you. What's a few more seconds? What's my actual blood being spilled? What's a little glass between friends?"

And this man-this man that was supposed to know me so well- kept his eyes on my hand and laughed. Laughed!

"Get off me." I said.

"In a second."

"Now."

"Cash-"

"-fucking now!" I snatched my hand away. The tweezers scratched over my palm. Who the fuck cared? I used one of our-his- fancy napkins to staunch the blood.

"What is your problem?" He had the audacity to actually sound and look confused. To back up like I was the one rooting around in his flesh for glass like I was on some kind of fucking treasure hunt.

Cute.

"If you don't know then I can't fucking tell you."

"That's not how any of this works, Cash."

"Yes. Because you make all the rules and I just show up and hope you'll stay with me or that your piece of rapist shit ex girlfriend doesn't pop up pregnant." That felt dramatic. Even for me. I liked it. "And hope that you won't leave me now because I have to be perfect mommy and perfect friend and perfect pussy and-"

"-I've never said you had to be any of those things."

"And you've never fucking told me that I didn't! You've never said that I'm enough."

"Yeah." He was quiet. In the face of my yelling and my body leaned over the table so that he had to look at me instead of the floor. His voice didn't raise. Not once. "I did. I have. And I will. I'm sorry you didn't hear me."

Excellent. "Don't give me some bullshit apology. Either you can really apologize or you can get the fuck out of my face."

"Okay." He went to kitchen counter, to the bowl where we kept our keys and picked up his. "Okay."

"Where are you going?"

"I need to walk away from this."

"No shit. I've been waiting for you to."

We were both still and let my words explode in the silence around us.

"There's bandages in the bathroom. Wash your hand out. Well." His fingers rubbed over his scars. "It's gonna hurt but pull the cut apart to make sure there's no glass left. It's not deep enough to need stitches. At least I don't think it is. But if it's still bleeding when I get back we'll go to the hospital. I'll tell your grandmother you're up here by yourself."

She didn't make a sound when I was yelling. And he didn't slam the door. But the minute it closed Olivia open her mouth and wailed like the world was ending.

Fuck.

CHAPTER THIRTEEN

Cahir

When I remembered it, it always felt like the arguing started at the same time that I really understood that I was adopted. There were never going to be pictures of my mother pregnant with me or in the hospital bed, exhausted and elated. There wasn't going to be exclamations that I looked more like one of them or the other.

There would be no mention of the personality traits I inherited from my grandparents. No hiding behind my parents. I would always be seen. It would always be obvious.

I thought they signed for me. Like a package. And like a package, I could be returned. They had all the paperwork. It would be easy to undo things. It would be easy to send me-not home. I didn't have that. I didn't have a point of origin. Just away. Away from everything I knew. I didn't quite understand wealth but I knew my life was easier. I knew I had things before I asked for them and my parents never said I couldn't have something because they couldn't afford it. I would never go to school on scholarship.

I didn't want to give up my life. I didn't want them to argue. But I couldn't make them stop.

They always did it at night. My father came home late. Too late, my mother screamed. He smelled like a distillery. He smelled like her.

I didn't know who "her" was and when I was old enough to understand, I didn't ask.

He was tired, he would say. Tired of the way she nagged him, the way she wanted more and more and more. He just wanted a little peace.

She laughed. No. My mother's laughter was kind and soft and made you feel like you'd just won Olympic gold. The sounds she made those nights made me feel like I was being stripped of everything I loved.

He wanted peace? That wasn't what he said when he chased her out of her first marriage. He said he wanted wild. He said he wanted untamed. He said he wanted to fuck her until she broke. Was he mad that he hadn't accomplished it? That she'd found his soft places and he'd never bothered with hers?

And more? Why in holy fuck shouldn't she want more? Her voice was so strong it made me wonder too as I hid under my covers. She'd left her home and everything she knew to come to America and help him chase a dream. She was the reason that dream came true. Or did he think he secured his promotions and later started his firm because he was just lucky? Did he think she hadn't gone out among those vapid, shallow women that couldn't see past their own implants to bring him business? Did he think he could do this without her? Oh, they could let the courts decide. She did that thing that wasn't a laugh. A divorce would be fun.

Night after night after night. Divorce, divorce, divorce.

She waited until the end to throw the word out. It meant I had to be silent when I cried so they wouldn't know. I couldn't give them another reason. I couldn't remind them that I was there. Better to shrink and be smaller and smaller.

They would forget I was there. Maybe they would forget until after the divorce was over and I could just hide where they were. Maybe they wouldn't mind that I was still around.

Eight months. I was quiet every night for eight months. One night I hiccuped and coughed and they went quiet. It was my father that found me. My father that held me as I sobbed in his lap and sent my mother away. My father that listened to me explain that when they weren't together it wouldn't matter to me. I didn't want to leave them. I would do whatever. I had been. Straight A's. I played whatever sport I thought he liked. Practiced until I was better than good and knew if I looked at the stands he would be there smiling. I helped my mother with dinner. I went with her to the grocery store. I read to her. I made her laugh with my impressions of her favorite actors. I watched her put on her makeup and told her every day that she was beautiful. Before my father could. If he did at all.

"So you don't have to send me back. I won't be in the way. I proved that. I can be good."

My father kissed my forehead and tucked me in. He told me he loved me. That would never change. He left my room. I saw my mother in the hallway. Her face was wet. The door was quiet when he closed it. So was he.

"There won't be a divorce. It's over now, Maeve."

And it was. I never heard them fight again. He made my mother smile at him. Then he made her laugh. And then one day she reached out to him, kissed him, in the middle of breakfast.

I didn't feel relieved. There was no room for it. I was too full of gratitude for my father. He saw the problem. He fixed it. He made sure I had a home.

CHAPTER FOURTEEN

Cassidy

I hated the feeling of the bandage on my hand. Hated the look on Gran's face when she came up the stairs to make sure I did right by my injury. The way she held my hand and turned it this way and that.

"You always did have a temper," she said. "Remember when you fought that girl that one summer?"

The first day of fashion camp. My stomach was in knots and that girl wouldn't stop looking at me, my shoes. I wore Payless because it was cute. Not because I didn't have a choice. I made sure she understood that.

"Or that teacher. What was her name?"

"Mrs. Wheeler."

"The way you tore that woman's classroom up." Gran chuckled. "Your father so proud of how you wouldn't back down when you knew you were right. Your mother sick of the both of you."

I smiled. "It wasn't my fault her classroom policies were so short-sighted."

Or that she didn't understand that I needed to walk away. The classroom was too warm, too close, and there was a boy. I'd seen him before. That day my body noticed him and I didn't understand how something that had always been in my control could disconnect from me so easily.

"Your mother figured it out first. Then me. We had to tell your father. You should have seen how he denied and then worried. Almost wore a path into the floor."

"What?"

"You, and your tantrums, and your fists, and your destruction. It only came when you were afraid. When you felt like you'd lost control and needed that fast way to get it back."

There was a time, long ago, when I argued with Gran. In that moment, I just held my breath while she poured peroxide over my hand.

"You won't need stitches. You can tell Cahir I said so. I won't be here when he comes back."

I rolled my eyes and yelped when she plucked me. Right on my cut.

"You're allowed to do what you want. That's what being grown means. You can set your life on fire and let it lead you down the path to hell if it'll make you smile." Her hand cupped my cheek. "Problem is it won't make you smile. You love him. Why can't you let yourself do that? What's the denial, and the holding back, and the anger getting you?"

"Way to fuck my night up."

She plucked me again and laughed when I hissed, kissed my cheek, kissed Olivia, and left.

I was on the couch when he came home hours later. Olivia slept on my chest. I was tired of keeping my eyes open. I wasn't worried about where he'd been. Who he'd seen. What he'd done. I did not compare my lack of reaction to Kevin, to the times he crept out in the middle of the night only to return in the morning and try to pretend as if he'd never left. I didn't think about it at all.

I ran my finger over Olivia's curls. I would treat her hair the way my mother did mine. Full of barrettes and beads and little braids that led nowhere and didn't make much sense in their placement. I would let her straighten it once a year, maybe twice. Her birthday and one other day of her choice. Like my mother, I would pretend I didn't see how excited she was, how she found any reason to move her head from one side to another. I'd brush and comb it and tell her that it didn't make her beautiful. No matter what she did she would be beautiful. But caring for her hair was caring for herself, a therapy Black women everywhere understood, embraced, and celebrated. I would teach her to love the way it grew out of her head, the way it defied logic, gravity, and what the world thought softness was. We would have that connection. In that way, we would be the same.

He sat on the coffee table and looked at Olivia and me. I wanted to ask what he saw, what he thought. Then he looked at my hand.

I didn't want anything but to go away. I didn't want to apologize.

"I can't do it anymore."

The apology rose up in me like bile. Maybe alongside it.

"I can't do the shouting and the arguing with you about shit that wouldn't have mattered a few months ago and doesn't really matter right now. Not with you. Not in front of her."

There was only shame. None of the jealousy that would have shown itself when we first brought Olivia home.

I didn't know what my father's raised voice sounded like until I was seventeen years old and went with him to a job site. I never heard my mother's voice rise above a conversational level. I didn't know what their anger looked like. They never directed it towards me. And there I was. I realized for the first time, for real, how much a baby changed everything.

"I want you. Not just as a friend or a coparent. As a life partner. As the person I do this thing with. If there were no Olivia, I would want that. You." He took a deep breath. "You aren't a replacement for Zion. I'm not biding my time or trying to bide my time until I can go back to her. You're it. It's you or it's no one. And, goddamn, I want to be with you."

It would be stupid to cry. I'd cried so much already. And I was finally feeling a little less tired.

"But I can't do it without you. I can't be with you unless you choose to stay. Like really stay. I'm not saying you're not gonna be scared sometimes. I'm just saying I'm going to be there when you are."

"Life partner?" It hurt to say but I couldn't hold the words and everything else inside.

"If I thought you were ready, I'd marry you tomorrow. Because you're you, and we're us, and it's never going to be better than what we have. Ever."

He didn't touch me, but I still felt him. Everywhere.

"I can't make you decide to stay though. I can't tell you what you want. Or how you should have it. I'm all in. You've gotta decide if you are too."

I nodded when I should have apologized.

"No matter what you decide though," he stood, "don't ever talk to me like that in front of our daughter again."

CHAPTER FIFTEEN

Cassidy

I thought he would leave me alone. I thought he would leave. His body would come home every night, the same as mine did. Whichever of us hadn't spent the day with Olivia would snatch her from her carrier and hold her, breathe her. It was me the first day. Me that held her and said thank you without knowing who the words were for.

He turned on music and grabbed me. Ignored my protests about the baby being sandwiched between us. We danced. Like we used to. The baby laughed. He smiled. He kissed me. We didn't talk about my tears. We just danced until they stopped.

Some days he sent Gran to pick up the baby. Or Nadia would walk into the office and fight with Delia about who would keep her for the night. O'Shea didn't argue. She scooped Olivia up and let Olivia rest over her belly. Walked away without a word. Sometimes she told me what time she would bring Olivia back. Cahir and I had drinks with Junie and decided, without looking at each other, that we wouldn't ask why Junie turned down every man that approached her and paid for her drinks with a credit card we hadn't seen before and didn't have her name on it.

He ran his thumb over my knuckles when we were alone in the car. "You know you can't ask her about it. You know what it's like to be asked something before you're ready to talk."

I waited until he laughed to hit his shoulder. I wanted to be sure.

He introduced me to Korean horror films. He laughed when I jumped. He held me as we laid in the bed, sheets and legs tangled together, and talked about what we watched. Capitalism and kindness and charity and bravery and how far we'd go for our family. We whispered dreams for Olivia into the comfortable dark. Dreams for ourselves. He talked in calm tones about the house he wanted. Quiet, gentle. Easy. Never too much. Never gave me a chance to forget that he wanted more with me and from me. One night I talked back. A pool and a balcony off my bedroom so I could see the sunrise while I had coffee or journaled. He could deal with Olivia. He laughed. He kissed me after I told him in that roundabout way that I didn't want to share a bed.

He took me out to dinner with my parents, Guy, and O'Shea and wasn't subtle about why we were there. My mother squealed and showed me houses she saved on her favorite realty app. She bickered with Guy about why her picks were better than anything he owned or worked on. O'Shea and my father whispered to each other about land laws, politics, and politicians. Why Baltimore was asa great place for business as the City and where they should go next. That was how the conversation ended- "they".

And I felt...warmer. There were days that the cracks

were more apparent than others, when I had to admit that it wasn't all getting better. Like the day I sat beside Cahir at the dining room table.

"I found a therapist. I went."

He put Olivia in her crib and came back to the table. He sat beside me instead of across from me. "How was it?"

"She said I'm allowed to feel crazy."

"You're allowed to feel whatever you want."

When was the last time I told him I loved him? I breathed for him? I looked for him before my eyes adjusted to the light? Reached for him before I fully left my dreams? "She said that trust is a mirror. But it's also a mosaic. She said broken pieces can be something beautiful if I make them."

"What do you think?"

"I think I want to see if she's right."

He kissed my forehead. "Okay."

∞

Cassidy

O'Shea was…pregnant. The kind of pregnant that made me uncomfortable when I saw her. Belly so big and what were once small breasts now so heavy. And a reminder. I felt like I'd always had Olivia but I looked at O'Shea and remembered it had only been about three months. I'd only lost my shit for about three months.

Wonderful.

"I need to talk to you," I said over the music.

She didn't turn. "Took you long enough."

I laughed. "It only took me an hour to work up the nerve."

"Nah. You've been working up the nerve for a while

now, Cassidy." She tucked a paintbrush into her locs. So much paint in her hair. "You've got a color. You know it?"

"Aura reading?" I sat at her worktable. "Gran did it for me once before she taught me."

"Fun." She smiled over her shoulder at me and rose. "I'm gonna mix it-your color. Tell me if I'm right when I'm finished."

She mixed. A warm green with depth but not dark.

"Yes," I said.

"Here's Cahir." She mixed together a rust orange.

"Yes." I didn't hold back my surprise. "Who are your people?"

She laughed. "Here's Zion."

She mixed a rich teal right next to my green. "It's why I didn't fight when he chose you and you decided to be his. Made sense to me. More sense than they did. Too dark for each other."

Zion's teal was swept off the table. A wet pop when it hit the concrete floor.

She mixed a paintbrush through Cahir and I's colors. "Let's paint."

"Right on the table?" I took the paintbrush she offered me.

"Guy will clean it later. He likes to clean while he fusses at me."

"What should we paint?"

"Don't worry about that. It'll be what it's going to be."

So I didn't. I just dragged color across the table. She cleared space for us on the table when it became clear that I needed it.

"I was angry with him. With me." I kept my eyes on our brushes. Hers lapped over mine. Brought definition. Additional colors. "I thought I was an idiot for going back to him. I thought I was being punished. For being too happy.

For having too much of a good thing. It always falls apart when I have too much of a good thing."

"The plight of the Black woman."

O'Shea and I snickered.

"I thought- I thought the baby would never look like me and that mattered. I told myself Olivia would always be more hers than mine and one day Cahir would realize it and leave."

"Mmm."

No judgment in the sound. I took a deep breath. "I was angry. That was all. Angry and ready for some kind of goddamned justice. It wasn't fair that he got his ready made family, and his smiles, and his beautiful kid and I had to be afraid."

"Keep painting. This is good." She dragged over a roll of canvas and pressed it into the wet paint. "The rest of the table. Come on. We're on a roll."

"Are you supposed to be carrying something that heavy?"

"No." Guy's drawl was always so pronounced.

So was the smile on O'Shea's face. "I knew you were coming to help me."

"Uh-huh. Give it here."

She tilted her face up. He kissed her. Dwarfed her. "I did. I could smell you."

"I believe that. I really do." He winked at me. "She smells everything now. You need me to go?"

"No." I shook my head. "You might help. I don't wanna get in your business but I heard-"

"-that his ex popped up with some delusional idea that she's gonna get him back. Child, yes. And getting rid of her hasn't even been fun. How come, do you think, no one wants to play with me?" O'Shea's question was for Guy, thankfully.

"Cause your playing involves low levels of cannibalism."
He wiped paint off her face and rubbed it into his pants.

"Are there levels to cannibalism?" I couldn't stop myself
from asking.

O'Shea smiled at me. "Ask your questions, baby."

"How do you deal with it? With the past always being
right there?"

She didn't look at me. Her eyes were on her husband.
"Nadia, right?"

"Nadia." He left and came back with her.

"Oh, no. I didn't mean to-" There were only so many
people that could hear my business and Nadia was a great
event planner and boss to Junie but...

"-this is what being a New Money Girl is." O'Shea
sighed a little when Guy settled her in his lap and Nadia
handed her a water. "Problem solving is a team sport. Plus I
can't answer your question."

"What's the question?" Nadia leaned on Guy and
rubbed O'Shea's stomach. Had I ever had friends like
that?

"How do you deal with the ex and the feelings," O'Shea
said.

"Oh." Nadia's gaze was sympathetic. "Do you have that
problem too, Cassidy?"

"You do?"

"Fine's ex." She waved a hand in front of her face.
"It's...happening."

"So I called in Nadia because we're both coming at this
from different angles, okay? I'm not worried about Guy
leaving me. He's made it abundantly clear that the only way
I'll get rid of him is to bury him."

"I picked out my plot," he said.

"Yes. It's a gorgeous piece of land in the middle of
nothing that will probably flood one day and have his body

floating up to our great-grandchildren's porch," O'Shea said.

"Probably." Guy nodded. "Keep life spicy."

We laughed.

"So honestly the only question I've got to answer is if I want her to live to see tomorrow and what continent do I think she should do it on," O'Shea said.

Guy and Nadia were relaxed. As if it were only the weather report.

Okay.

"Nadia has to deal with feelings," O'Shea said.

"Mine and his," Nadia said.

"Okay," I said.

"The first thing I had to do was pull my head out of my behind and get honest with myself. Right? They had feelings for each other. Did I want to be angry? Did I want to cry? Did I want to have his ex investigated and followed?"

The small blessing was that I hadn't even considered those things as options.

"I didn't want that," Nadia said. "I just wanted him. That was a turning point. Admitting that I wanted to stay. I wanted to fight. I've never fought before. I've never had to."

I nodded.

"Fighting isn't even physical really," she said. "I'm going to do some of that."

"I can't wait." O'Shea rubbed her hands together.

"Yeah, you can," Guy said.

"It's more psychological. And it's all mine. Do I believe him? When he says he wants me do I believe him? Do I believe myself when I say I want to stay? Do I believe that my fears aren't justified and need to be dealt with when they present themselves? Do I know that fear happens? Do I know it's okay? Do I recognize when it controls my actions? When it makes things worse?"

I wouldn't cry, I told myself.

"Most important: if the fear becomes reality, if he leaves, will I be okay? Am I strong enough, just me, to make it in a world without him? If the answer to that is no then it doesn't matter what he does, I'm never going to get this right."

I don't know who handed me the tissues. I was just grateful they didn't ask me why I cried.

CHAPTER SIXTEEN

Cassidy

A week later. My day to have Olivia at work with me. We liked to dress within the same color story. To take pictures before anyone else showed up. Just for us. My clients asked why she didn't have a social media. Why I didn't take advantage of having a beautiful, happy baby.

"Some things are just for us," I said.

I changed the music until I found something she bounced her little body to. Cahir said that objectively she wasn't clapping. I disagreed and sent him video to prove it.

An early feeding. A diaper change. A little whispering between the two of us. She rested easy in my lap while I meditated. She smiled at my clients. They knew not to ask to hold her.

I only put her down to take photographs. Then one of my clients brought me fabric and taught me how to twist and turn it to create a sling that kept Olivia close to my heart.

She still fussed sometimes. I understood. Sometimes I wanted to sit by myself too.

That day I peeled the fabric back to look down on her. "It's okay. Mommy's here."

She settled. Drifted off to sleep.

And I stood, camera in my hand, and repeated my words back to myself over and over and over.

Not a single tear fell.

∞

Cahir

She went to therapy once a week. She meditated every morning instead of going straight to the baby. She did things alone.

"I'm going for a walk," she said one night. Except she didn't walk. She hovered by the door with a vice grip on her keys. She stared at me, wild-eyed.

"Okay. Enjoy your walk."

She nodded and a minute or so later she left. That first walk was short.

"I'm going shopping with Junie," she said one Saturday.

"Okay. Take my card."

She put on a fashion show when she came back and I was the reason she didn't get out of the bed for anything but the bathroom, food, and the baby for the next sixteen hours.

Over dinner a few days later: "The guys are doing that brunch thing, right?"

I nodded.

"You should go." She looked at me. "I want you to go."

Not that brunch lasted long. O'Shea's water broke as soon as things got interesting.

A few days later:

"Did you want to go to the movies tonight?"

I held still. "Who's gonna take-"

"Gran. She's complaining. She said Olivia should be learning how to run the shop."

I smiled. "She's smart enough."

"So?" She didn't meet my eyes and twisted her fingers.

Did she think I could ever say no to her? "No horror." She smiled at me.

She smiled at me a lot. We didn't talk too much about it. But she smiled. And then she laughed. And then she reached for my hand. Not my naked body in quiet early morning when it's easier to pretend. My hand. Before she got out of the car.

One day she led me to the couch and sat down. Her legs draped over my thighs. I thought about the first time she did that. The first time I realized we could be comfortable. And the day that changed everything for us, up on the Lonely Third.

It was my father that taught me life, history, existence, all of it was circular. What we released came back. What went around came back around. And the most important part of any journey was the beginning. The most important part of any relationship was the foundation it was built on.

I found myself grateful that Cash and I had magic nights, sloppy cheesesteaks, designer suits, dance floors, and tables too small for our food, our drinks, our elbows, before we had kisses and bodies pressed tight.

"So. Therapy." She kept her hand in mine. Steady. "I've been in for a while."

"You've done your bid with real courage and forbearance."

She threw her head back and laughed. "Shut up."

"I could try."

"Or you could just do."

"You have great legs." It wasn't the point, and I didn't want anything but to see her smile again.

She did. "I'm glad I went to therapy. It…helps to have someone that doesn't know me hear about my problems and tell me I'm not crazy in a way that isn't fixable."

I nodded.

"I didn't want to fix it. That was the hardest part. To admit that there was part of me that liked wallowing. There was a part of me that just wanted to drown in self-pity at all the things that happened to me."

Her voice was low, introspective. There wasn't enough room in my chest for my lungs.

"It wasn't a lot of fun. It didn't make me happy. It kept me from Olivia. I want to be her mother." She pushed her hair away from her face. "I want you to know that."

"I do."

"I am her mother." Her smile was blinding. "I know that. And I know that I have absolutely no idea what I'm doing even though I watched all those videos online and read those books and listened to the podcast."

"I found a documentary."

"We're going to watch it." She nodded. "I have no idea what I'm doing, and that's okay. It doesn't mean I can't figure it out and be good at this."

"I don't know what I'm doing either."

"Oh, I definitely know that." She yelped when I poked her in the side. "I don't think you're going to leave me."

The laughter was gone. I liked what replaced it.

"I don't think I've ever thought it. I think I just-grounding, my therapist calls it. She said we have to ground ourselves in some kind of reality and our subconscious brain doesn't care what type of reality it is as long as there's a framework that dictates how we react to the world around us."

"You needed a world where I'd walk out on you."

"I needed a world that gave me reasons to hide. I'm coming out of that world. By being selfish of all things." She laughed.

"Tell me about it."

"I- you know how when you get on a plane they tell you that you have to put on your own mask before you can help someone else?"

"Yeah."

"That."

"That's it?"

"You've never needed a lot of words to understand what I'm trying to say."

No. Another kind of miracle that existed between us.

CHAPTER SEVENTEEN

Cassidy

There were clothes on the bed for me. Just before the sun was up. A chipped coffee mug with flowers in it. A little piece of citrine. For hope. I was glad he was my friend. I was glad, while I breathed in wild flowers and their elegant, greenhouse grown cousins, to have a man that saw my world and dove into it. Absorbed so much of me and still stayed him. A quiet miracle but not a small one.

I showered and dressed. I made breakfast and coffee while he dressed the baby. He put her in her stroller and grabbed the basket. The farmer's market basket.

I thought the smile would crack my face open. I thought the joy would crack each of my ribs. Clean cuts because it was so powerful and so unable to be contained. He took the basket and I pushed the stroller over the cracks in the sidewalk and I talked to him. About work and maybe a trip. Maybe we should take Olivia on a trip.

"Why not? We don't fly commercial."

I stood still for a moment and marveled at how casually he could sum up how my life had changed and what my daughter's would be.

My daughter. Gran's friends smiled wider when they saw us. Gave us drinks and advice and looked to me.

They looked at me. "Give me your baby."

"Let me see your baby girl."

"May refuses to bring her granddaughter to meet us. Took you long enough."

"Oh, look at your beautiful baby!"

"Look at all those cheeks."

"Look at them arms. Just wanna eat her up."

"She's gonna have hair like you and May. Y'all always got to show off with all that pretty hair."

And the best one. "She looks like her daddy. Bet she acts like you."

Yes. She did. Or she didn't. Either way-

Vegetables and more succulents. It was me that protested. His apartment overflowed with them. Mine did too.

"Give them away." He shrugged. "And there are no plants at Beyond. All that space on the Lonely Third."

I hadn't-Why hadn't I considered that?

"Okay. That's enough," he said thirty minutes later after he pried his credit card out of my hand. "Let's go, Poison Ivy."

"Oh my God. That's who I should be for Halloween!"

"I don't think I would make a very good Harley Quinn."

I laughed so loud everyone around us went silent. And I didn't stop. Until I was good and goddamned ready. Until Olivia stopped kicking and laughing along with me.

∞

Cahir

She was absolutely the same and totally different. The most familiar part of my life and a strange new thing. It was in the way her hips swayed when we danced. Full circles, full of time, and perfectly in synch with the beat of the music and her heart. It was in her laugh. The way she spoke. Lower, quieter, fuller. With comfort and a promise that she wasn't going anywhere. Silky in a way that didn't disturb thoughts or a baby's sleep.

She was...anticipatory. There to answer before I'd fully formed the question. There to laugh before the joke. To moan before I took off her clothes. Softer. She leaned on me more. An easy reminder of how strong she was.

Getting to know her again forced me to relearn myself. And made it obvious I needed to go shopping.

∞

Cassidy

There was only one thing we hadn't talked about. Crazy. We'd talked about so many other things. Poked, and probed, and prodded at the new places we found since the elevator, since Olivia came to us.

The house. Two bedrooms.

I didn't talk about it but I thought about it. Every second. Every time I woke up next to him and stayed quiet. To hear him breathe. To feel the way he pressed against me no matter how hot our bodies got or how quickly his arm or my leg fell asleep.

I knew it was there. An app on his phone where he collected real estate listings. Emails from Guy and my father about places that might work. Neighborhoods.

Schools and their ratings. Articles that debated schools and homeschooling. I loved him for it. That he planned for us and had the patience to wait for me to speak.

I didn't know why I stayed silent. Anxiety? Fear? My therapist told me to follow it. To explore it.

It was fear that I found. Fear that I once again misread the signs. That I once again overestimated our progress, our bond, and would soon be standing in his office again. Asking why he was gone. Running.

I was stronger. I found my strength beside the fear. Smiled at how they were entwined together. Co-dependent in their own way. And Olivia demanded that I be better.

I held her while I made coffee for me and Cahir. I hummed to her. On key. Dances to match.

I almost tripped when I heard his laugh. Silly. "Good morning."

He kissed me. Then Olivia. "Is this for me?"

"Since you didn't brush your teeth."

He laughed again. Morning breath drowned by coffee and him underneath it all.

"I wanted to talk to you about something," I said.

The conversation would have been easier if he weren't shirtless. If he didn't lean against the counter with that coffee cup and look like every bad decision I was glad I made.

"Cash."

I heard the smile before I saw it. I looked away. Deep breath. *Do it, Cassidy.*

"I've been thinking about the house." I felt the laughter flee. I wanted to do the same, but I'd started. I had to finish. "Can we house shop? I have a list of things I want."

"You'll have it."

"All of it?"

"Whatever you want."

"If what I want is a big bedroom?"

"Yeah. You can have the biggest one."

"And if I want to share that big bedroom with you?"

An audible sigh. A heavy sigh. A release of something and preparation for another thing. "Look at me, Cash."

I did. And wished I hadn't. "We don't-"

"Good. Because we won't. We're not going house shopping. Not like this."

Olivia fussed against my chest. I loosened my arms. Gave her room to move. To breathe.

Cahir walked away from me. Into the closet. And I stood frozen in place. A fool again. A fool for him. That was fine. I wouldn't wet my daughter's hair with my tears. I would move back into my apartment. We would figure out a custody schedule. And we would figure out what the hell was wrong with him and fix it. Eventually, we would be the family we were meant to be. The idiot wouldn't escape me for-

"If we're going to shop for a house," he dropped to one knee and held up an open ring box, "you're going to have to wear this."

"You-" It was beautiful. He was beautiful. And I was a liar- I was getting my daughter's hair wet with my tears.

"I am going to love you every day for the rest of my life and I want you and the world to see it, know it, recognize it." He smiled. "All of that. Say you'll do it. Say you'll marry me."

"Yes." I said over and around my tears. "Of course I will."

Olivia's little hands bounced off my chest and cheeks, her sweet, baby laughs in my ear, as Cahir slid the ring on my finger.

All five novels in the New Money Girls series in one place!

Tony and LeAndra

Belong to Me

Will king pin Tony quit the game for love? Will wealthy LeAndra give up her world to become a part of his? When their worlds collide sparks fly but so do tempers.

Conquer with Me

There's blood on her hands and at his feet. Can Tony and LeAndra rebuild their lives and the love they once shared?

Rule with Me

Can two lost souls find their way back to love and live life the way they'd planned: happily together?

Tony and LeAndra: The Complete Series Box Set

All three novels in the Tony and LeAndra series in one place!

Cassidy and Cahir

Better as Friends

He's strictly off limits. His ex ruined his life. Before he can move on I have to be sure his past is truly behind him.

Better than Your Ex

She lost him. She thinks it's over. She doesn't know that he's coming for her, that she's the love of his life.

Better as Lovers

He agreed to give her time. She agreed to stay by his side. Can the couple who had a bright future ahead of them, find their way past the obstacles and build a better future together or is it too late?

Friends to Lovers: The Complete Cassidy and Cahir Series

All three novels in the Cassidy and Cahir series in one place!